Of Eternal Life

Micah Persell

CRIMSON
ROMANCE
Avon, Massachusetts

Published by
Crimson Romance
an imprint of F+W Media, Inc.
10151 Carver Road, Suite 200
Blue Ash, Ohio 45242

www.crimsonromance.com

DEDICATION

FOR SHANNON
YOU KNOW WHY—THE REASONS ARE TOO NUMEROUS
TO MENTION HERE.

Acknowledgments

Thank you to my first readers, Lord Chuck and Stoney-poo. This book wouldn't even have made it off the ground without your expertise and friendship.

Thank you to Mom and Dad for raising me to love reading and writing.

Thank you to my husband for understanding all those times you've asked me a question, and I haven't responded because I've been plotting a scene in my mind. I wouldn't know romance without you, hon.

And, finally, thank you to my amazing editor, Jennifer. You saw the story I was trying to tell and showed me how to write it. I'll be eternally grateful for your guidance.

The Lord God made all kinds of trees grow out of the ground—trees that were pleasing to the eye and good for food. In the middle of the garden were the tree of life and the tree of the knowledge of good and evil.

Genesis 2:8-9

Chapter One

Abilene Miller, sitting cross-legged on the floor, squinted at the rolls of gauze on the shelf in front of her through the fringe of her lashes. When the gauze blended into something resembling a snow-covered mountain, she sighed with satisfaction and leaned her head back against the wall behind her. The supply closet was the coolest place in the hospital, and with this little trick, she could almost fool herself into thinking she was *not* in the God-forsaken Mojave Desert.

"Southern California, you lying bitch," she murmured as she took a vehement bite from her peanut butter and jelly sandwich.

Dreams of rolling ocean waves, vibrant night life, and Disneyland had quickly given way to the reality that was Needles, California: a small town of 4,000 outside of the Mojave National Preserve.

Of course, the two military recruiters who had come to her hometown of Aspen, Colorado, right after med school to convince her to come work in their "cutting edge" research facility had played up those very tourist attractions in a way that merited a court martial for perjury. If that was even a thing that could happen. She didn't know. *Military I am not*, she thought in amusement as she set aside her sandwich for a baggie of Oreos.

She sighed again, this time in disgust. *Top 5 percent of my class at Duke University Medical School, and I get duped.* She hadn't even begun her residency, and these guys had wanted her. Really, *really* wanted her. Enough to throw an obscene amount of money at her, making "no" an impossibility. And if she had thought it was suspicious that they wanted to hire her before she had even seen the facility, the pull of finally being on her own had overshadowed the oddity.

She snorted. "On her own" was proving to be an elusive concept. In fact, she felt as though every step she took was measured. She lived in a military dormitory with the four other women who worked in the labs. They all carpooled to work each morning, and the head of the hospital, Major Taylor, seemed to lurk around every corner, as aware of her movements as her overbearing parents.

Abilene knew she'd made a mistake in taking this job. She just so badly needed to prove herself. What was that old adage? If it sounds too good to be true, don't effing move into a military compound?

"Abilene, you in here?"

She gave an unfeminine grunt in response and returned her attention to her Oreos. The door edged open, and Dahlia looked in.

"Oh, Abi, hon, are you fantasizing that the gauze is snow again?"

"Among other things," Abilene replied.

Dahlia shut the door behind her and sank down to the floor beside Abilene, reaching over and snagging an Oreo from the baggie. She turned her warm caramel-colored eyes toward Abilene.

"Tough day?"

Abilene met her friend's gaze. "Dahlia, how many patients have you seen today?"

Understanding lit in her friend's eyes. Dahlia had been at the facility longer than Abilene. She had been recruited straight out of the University of Pennsylvania, also before her residency, and had been working here for nearly ten months. From their talks, Abilene knew it had been a *long* ten months.

"Abi, I haven't seen any patients today. You know that."

Abilene nodded. Both women had come to this hospital in part because they believed in the cause. According to the military recruitment team that had visited each of them, the government was conducting an experiment in which they planned to refurbish small, abandoned military buildings in rural areas. These facilities would be for the local population as well as for the processing of the armed forces' medical tests. The facilities would employ civilian doctors, but they would be funded by the government and sanctioned by the military.

It was nice in theory; however, the largely Native American population in Needles viewed any help from the government with suspicion, understandably so, and avoided the new hospital as though they still used plague-ridden blankets—a reaction the government had to have expected, which lead Abilene to wonder what the real purpose of this facility was. It was hard to believe she and the other women were here just to run labs.

"What are we *doing* here?" Abilene pushed a hand through her short blonde curls in frustration. "Damn it, I want to see patients. I want to save lives. I want to do *something*." Dahlia broke eye contact and looked at the floor.

Abilene blew out a breath. "Sorry." She offered a smile. She'd gotten carried away again. "Jeez, I'm sorry, Dahlia. I know you're frustrated, too."

Dahlia gave Abilene's knee a squeeze. "Hey," she shrugged, "the government is paying us to run labs and make friends. What's to complain about?" She rose to her feet in effortless grace, turning to offer Abilene a hand up. "Come on. Treat you to a Diet Coke from the vending machine?"

This was turning into a tradition among the women at the hospital. Whenever one of them had a meltdown, it always ended with Diet Coke, which, personally, Abilene loathed. The other women sucked it down like ambrosia.

"Oh baby, you know just what I like," Abilene said in a breathy voice, grasping Dahlia's proffered hand while shoving thoughts of her disappointing career aside. She rose to her feet, much less gracefully than Dahlia. "You and your weird *Swan Lake* moves suck, you know," she grumbled.

Dahlia chuckled and glided out into the hall.

***

Awareness flooded his senses so quickly he choked on his gasp of air. For several moments all he could do was gulp as his body took over in its need for oxygen. His lungs burned. He could hear his ragged breaths echoing around him, bouncing around an empty cavern.

Where am I?

His instinct urged him to take in any details he could. He heard a measured beep. His frantic mind wouldn't place it. In fact, he couldn't seem to concentrate on anything but that hysterical pull of air. Panic crept into the edges of his consciousness, causing his heart rate to thump.

Where was he? What was happening? Why was he . . . *afraid?*

God, not fear.

His mind clamped down on him. Fear was dangerous.

Regulate breathing. Determine surroundings. He clenched his teeth behind closed lips. Slowly, steadily, he drew a measured breath through his nose. The debilitating fear in his chest abated. *Again*, an internal voice whispered."

He pulled another breath through flared nostrils, this time blowing it out between parted, parched lips. As the panic receded, he noticed the incessant beeping slowed. In an instant, he discerned the beeping: his own heart rate.

A medical facility.

I'm hurt? He took mental inventory of his body. The sudden awareness of his limbs brought an onrush of pain. His bones felt crushed, agony knifed through him, and he groaned in the back of his throat.

Pain. Familiar pain. He was not a stranger to this anguish. He eased his eyes open. An involuntary moan escaped his lips, and he squeezed his eyes shut against the bright lights.

"1457, subject is stirring. Shows signs of light-related visual pain."

Intense, animal fear arose at the sound of the clinical voice above his head. At the alarming reference to a *subject*.

As in test subject? Ah, God . . .

He held his breath as he processed this new information, what the presence of that voice meant.

I'm not alone.

For some reason, instead of calming him, this revelation ratcheted the terror tighter, to the snapping point. The inner voice whispered urgently: *This man is dangerous.*

A lock fell from a hidden cache of information in his brain. He recognized the voice that whispered to him. The Voice had been his constant companion since this nightmare had begun. Now, the Voice whispered the identity of the other person in the room: *The Tormentor.*"

This involuntary movement caused more pain to slice through him, and he just stopped another moan from rising out of his chest. He could not let himself make any sounds of distress. Another revelation from that hidden instinct: *Hide your suffering. He* loves *it.*

Oh, God. How did he know that? There was no doubt in his mind that he knew that from personal experience. This newest revelation solved his fight-or-flight dilemma: flight.

He moved his left arm infinitesimally to determine how much pain he would be dealing with when he fled. He became aware of the cold, cutting metal impeding further movement.

A new flare of panic. *Oh, no. Not that.* He moved his arm again and met the same immovable restraint. He tried to move his feet. He was shackled. The sharp edges of the metal binding his wrists and ankles bit into his skin, adding to the buffet of pain, but his terror would not allow him to cease his struggles.

His mind screamed at him, urging his body to do the impossible.

"1500, subject is showing usual onset of panic at regained consciousness. Thrashing has opened wounds at the sites where he is restrained."

The last of his confusion melted away. He remembered. He remembered *everything*, and knew he was lost. There would be no escape, just as there had been no escape for the past eight years. He'd been through this before. The panicked awakening. The fierce pain swamping every corner of his existence. The dawning horror of remembered tortures.

When he forced his eyes open, ignoring the sting of the bright operating room lights, a familiar figure approached.

"Always such a fuss, hmm, Eli?" The Tormentor tsked. Eli recoiled. His name was not safe with that man. He never heard it without being reminded that he had no control over himself or his situation.

His struggles against the metal restraints now resulted in a rather satisfying cacophony, but still only caused blood to drip down his arms and pool beneath his feet. The Tormentor approached, eyeing the damage Eli had done to himself with a sadistic leer that turned Eli's stomach.

"Blood is strength, you know." The Tormentor shook his head in mock-sorrow. "What a pity that you seem to hold it in such low regard."

A feral growl resonated in Eli's chest, and he punched his head up from the stretcher to glare into the Tormentor's eyes. "I'm going to kill you. I'm going to make sure everyone knows what you've done here, and then," he paused to ensure the Tormenter was looking at him, "I'm going to kill you."

The Tormentor cocked an eyebrow and raised a recording device to chin level. "0817, subject is displaying the symptoms of aggression that have heretofore been associated with memory recollection. Has threatened death. Again." He clicked off the recording device and slipped it into the pocket of his scrubs.

"'What I've done here,' hmm?" He leaned down until his face almost touched Eli's. "What I've done here is what you signed up for, soldier. Nothing more, nothing less." He straightened with a sneer and turned toward the door.

One of the two guards on the other side of the see-through barrier keyed a code into the door, and the hiss of released pressure and a grinding of gears announced that the door was unlocked. The Tormentor paused with his hand on the handle and turned to announce over his shoulder, "Number 140 begins in four hours. Perhaps you should use this time to gather your strength instead of waste it." He twisted the handle and left the room.

Four hours.

In just four hours they were going to conduct their one hundred fortieth experiment.

Number 14: gunshot wound to the chest. The cold feel of steel pushed against his sternum. The force of the bullet driving his body into the unforgiving metal at his back. Gunpowder stinging his nostrils as his teeth chattered from the cold caused by his bleeding out.

Number 58: asphyxiation by smothering. Excruciating burning in his lungs. The flailing of his limbs as he fought the restraints in a need to knock the oppressive hand from his mouth and nose. Stars dotting his vision as his brain fought the lack of oxygen.

His heart rate sped up to match his ragged breathing. *Number 100: dismemberment.* He couldn't stifle the moan that memory dredged up, hearing in his mind the buzz of the bone saw, feeling the heat of whirring metal on flesh. His Tormentor had informed him that they had wanted to make the one hundredth "special."

He was panting like an animal now. *Four hours.* In four hours, they were going to kill him.

For the one hundred fortieth time.

Chapter Two

The heavy thump of men's dress shoes brought all five women's heads up from their lab work. Lisa and Mary exchanged an almost girly giggle as the door swung open and Major Taylor poked his blond head in.

Major Taylor slipped into the room. The overhead lights gleamed off his clean-cut good looks. One dimple formed as he smiled hello. All of the females seemed to melt into the stools surrounding the black slab table. Major Taylor noticed, a cocky grin appearing in response. Abilene fought a groan of annoyance. They were single-handedly setting back women's rights by about fifty years.

"Ah, ladies, you're all here."

Okay, Abilene had to admit he *did* have a pretty sigh-worthy voice. It was smooth and deep and resonant. Lisa and Mary practically fanned themselves with their lab coats, and Dahlia exchanged a wink with Olive. Abilene couldn't restrain the smile their antics brought and bent her head to her petri dish to keep it from the advancing Major.

"Everything okay in here?" he asked, coming to rest beside Abilene's stool. His broad shoulders, paired with his height, blocked out her light, and she squinted up at his haloed silhouette.

He surveyed her work with an approving crinkle of his dark eyes, not once gazing at the others' labs. His obvious partiality made Abilene squirm in her seat.

Her coworkers were accomplished women. Lisa and Olive had been in the same class at Johns Hopkins. Dahlia came from the University of Pennsylvania, and Mary was top of her class at Harvard. In comparison, Abilene was the dregs of the group, yet Major Taylor doted on her. Abilene wasn't even trying anymore, and she still won his approval. Too bad *his* approval was not fulfilling.

"Um, yes, sir, everything's great." From across the table Dahlia gave her an encouraging smile.

"What are we working on today?"

Her mind went blank as she scrambled for an answer. What *was* she working on? *Ah, jeez.* She gazed frantically at the dish in her hand and waited for lightening to strike. Suddenly the answer was there, and she blurted out her findings as soon as her mind grasped them.

"It looks like Private Alvarez has gonorrhea." She cringed. "Sir," her voice cracked mid-word.

Shit.

She winced as she met Dahlia's wide eyes and saw Olive cover her mouth. Lisa and Mary's mouths were slack in disbelief.

A half dozen other diagnoses in front of me, and I report that one.

"Ah, yes, well." Major Taylor cleared his throat and took a measured step back from Abilene and the offending petri dish. "Poor Private Alvarez." He moved to the end of the table and used his best grin on each of the women.

"Well, ladies, we have another drill scheduled for 1200, so when you leave for lunch, go ahead and take the rest of the day off." He threw a wink in Lisa and Mary's direction, "Have a little fun."

Abilene frowned, and the women met each other's eyes. They'd had a drill three weeks ago when she first came to the hospital. In all of that time Abilene had seen exactly zero patients, spending her days running tedious labs and mailing results out to military bases. Who could they be running drills for?

There's no one here.

What were they hiding when the civilians cleared the building? Weapons?

Major Taylor seemed to sense the direction of her thoughts.

"It's for the military personnel here at the hospital. No need for you to be worried," he said. Ah, this she was used to. Her short crop of blond curls, big blue eyes, and freckled nose often elicited this don't-worry-your-pretty-little-head response from macho men. God, she *hated* that. But at least it ensured that they underestimated her ninety percent of the time.

Not that she'd ever proved to them that they had underestimated her. But there was always a first time. She just knew it.

"Of course not," she assured in her best big-girl voice, which only made Major Taylor's smile soften even more.

"Okay, I'll let you all get back to what you're doing." He eyed the petri dish still balanced in the palm of Abilene's hand. "Keep up the good work." He strode through the door, closing it behind him.

One . . . two . . .

"Oh, Abilene," Olive burst out as Lisa and Mary started laughing, "you're my hero."

"Yay," Abilene mumbled under her breath as she finally set down her petri dish.

"I'm starting a fan club right now. Ladies," Olive turned to Lisa, Mary, and Dahlia, "care to join? Dues are only drinks at lunch."

"Honey," Dahlia interjected as she made her way to Abilene's side, "I've already founded that club. *You* can pay the dues to *me*." She squeezed Abilene's shoulder as she whispered for her ears only, "It's okay. You were cute."

"Yeah, *that's* going to get me far in the medical field." She turned to the others. "How soon do you think we can leave for lunch?"

Dahlia looked at the clock on the wall. "An hour. Come on," she tugged at Abilene's arm. "Diet Coke?" Olive, Mary, and Lisa clapped their hands in enthusiasm and jumped up and down like little kids. Abilene felt her lips tug up in a reluctant smile, recognizing their Valley-girl act as an attempt to cheer her up.

"Diet Coke can't solve every problem, you know," she felt obliged to point out.

Lisa gasped as Mary dramatically whispered, "Blasphemy!"

"Hey, Duke, I thought you were supposed to be smart," accused Olive.

A genuine chuckle burst from Abilene's lips. "You're right. I don't know what I was thinking." As she headed out the door she said, "Diet Cokes on me, girls."

***

The rasp of a razor bounced off the unfinished stone walls as an orderly shaved Eli's chin and cheeks. That his lower face had to be hairless for whatever was going to occur made Eli's stomach twist in anxiety.

What was it to be this time? The Tormentor relished suspense, saving the revelation of what was to kill him until the very last possible moment. He played a sick version of Twenty Questions with Eli, revealing symptom after symptom that he was soon to experience until Eli could either guess what was coming or—the Tormentor's favorite—the focus of the experiment was whispered into Eli's ear.

A smooth jaw meant one thing: they needed something to seal over his mouth or both his mouth and nose. *Ingestion.* He felt himself relax by a degree. If he had to swallow something, then that meant he could fight it. Never mind that his efforts had always been overcome in the past; he was a man, damn it, and a trained one at that. He would fight with all the strength in his body if it were the only victory allowed him in this hellish place.

The door's hiss and whir announced the Tormentor's entrance into the roo"It's a beautiful day today, Eli. Bright blue skies, gentle breeze." He flicked a negligent glance over the orderly's progress and returned his gaze to the clipboard he was carrying. "I might head toward the coast for a bit." He paused, enjoying his captive audience. "After."

Eli jerked his arms in his restraints. Hell, what he wouldn't give to pound that smirk from the Tormentor's horrid face. "Yuk it up,

Doc," he growled. "How long do you think this can continue?" You're a pathetic man who gets his rocks off on keeping another man at his mercy. You'll slip up. Someday you'll make a mistake, and when you do," he bared his teeth, "you're mine."

The Tormentor showed no reaction. "Any idea of what we have planned for you today?"

"Fuck you."

The Tormentor chuckled, "No? Come now. Smart one like you, you must have some clue." He circled around Eli's stretcher, maintaining eye contact all the while. "There's the prep from the orderly. . . ."

Eli refused to give an inch in this battle of wills. He glared into the Tormentor's eyes and ground his jaw, a muscle ticking in his cheek.

The Tormentor tsked. "That's okay, I'm feeling sporting today. How about a clue, hmm?" He made the circuit to Eli's head and leaned over him. "Two to three hours." He cocked his head like an animal to better gauge any telltale flickers of realization on Eli's face.

Fuck.

Poison. He'd known that had to be it when he'd figured out the ingestion part. He steeled his features, revealing nothing, but his chin jerked up in defiance and the Tormentor noticed.

"Ah, we're getting warmer, I see," he cajoled.

Eli's brain was scrambling. Two to three hours was pretty damn fast for a poison he would have to swallow. In just this moment he could think of maybe three poisons that would fit the bill. Cyanide, lye—

The Tormentor leaned closer and whispered, "Convulsions."

Strychnine. Eli's mouth went dry.

"Well, well," the Tormentor straightened in disappointment. "That wasn't so difficult, was it?"

Oh, God, Eli's heart stuttered in his chest. Strychnine was a horrible way to die. The victim literally convulsed to death, his body contorting painfully as his muscles fought oncoming doom. And the best part? He'd be aware the whole time, completely cognizant of his surroundings, of his agony, until his body finally gave out.

The snap of latex gloves ricocheted off the walls like a shot, and the Tormentor impatiently beckoned the orderly carrying a tray to come forward. "Since there's no more fun to be had in that little game, we may as well begin directly."

Eli refused to crane his head around to watch the preparations. He'd learned that early on. Knowing every detail about what was to come only made it worse. It was bad enough that he now knew Number 140 was Strychnine poisoning; he wouldn't threaten his tenuous control with more knowledge.

"1200, proceeding with experiment Number 140: Strychnine poisoning. Prepping patient for introduction of toxin." The Tormentor moved to one side of Eli's head and motioned the orderly to the other side, "Open his mouth."

A warm, latex-covered hand gripped Eli's chin while another covered his nose while grasping his cheeks. Eli gritted his mouth closed. When the burning in his lungs grew too great, he puffed air through his clenched teeth and parted lips, but he refused to open his mouth. The orderly grew more aggressive, covering his nose and mouth now, cutting off even that small amount of oxygen.

Eli thrashed he head, but he was unable to shake the orderly from him. The burning in his lungs grew. And grew. His whole body jerked in protest, and his head kicked back as he gasped against the latex covering his mouth. In that second of surrender, the orderly removed his hand, and the Tormentor thrust clear plastic tubing into the side of Eli's mouth and all the way to the back of his throat while the orderly worked a splint between his teeth. The hard scrape of the tubing against the roof of his mouth caused him to gag.

"Uh-uh," the Tormentor scolded as the orderly taped the tubing into place. "None of that." He returned to his recorder, "1204, administering the toxin."

The Tormentor lifted the open ending of the tubing to shoulder height and flourished a beaker filled with cloudy liquid past Eli's face. "It's a grand way to die, you know," he said. "According to legend, it's what got Alexander the Great. You could do much worse than to share something this intimate with such an accomplished ruler."

The orderly eyed the Tormentor over Eli's head. Eli was not the only one who noticed the unholy delight the Tormentor took in these actions. Weak prey always seemed to know when a dangerous predator was nearby.

The orderlies quit and had to be replaced often. It didn't take long for the lies the Tormenter told them about Eli's past to become less-appalling to them than the Tormentor's own actions.

Eli had no idea what happened to those who quit, but he couldn't imagine the Tormentor ever letting them go.

The Tormentor grimaced at the orderly's scrutiny and moved the lip of the beaker to the tubing. Eli's eyes followed the movement of liquid from beaker to tube and down toward his mouth with alarm. The tubing ensured fighting would be unsuccessful. Why hadn't he foreseen this possibility?

The moment the liquid hit the back of Eli's mouth he gagged anew, this time at the taste. It was *bitter*. Metallic. If death could have a taste, this would be it.

The orderly covered Eli's nose again, and he knew he was screwed. He would swallow it; his body would demand its own doom in a quest for life-giving air.

Even knowing this, Eli struggled until his throat gulped convulsively. The poison burned all the way into his gut, and his hacking coughs rang out over the snick of the recorder being turned on.

"1208, toxin administered successfully." The Tormentor settled on a utilitarian stool at Eli's shoulder and eyed him expectantly as the orderly removed the splint and tubing. "Now," he sighed, "we wait."

Chapter Three

Eli's back bowed off of the stretcher, the entire weight of his jerking body resting on his shoulders and heels. His facial muscles tightened in a soundless scream as his toes curled under his feet.

The convulsions had begun just five minutes after he'd swallowed the poison, starting in his neck and face. Over the last two hours they'd increased in intensity and frequency until he was suffering episodes like this. Excruciating stretches of agony that caused him to wish for death as soon as they ended.

This one was lasting longer than he thought he could survive. *Oh, God, let it end. Let this be it.* He was finally able to wrench his mouth open, and his scream rent the air, increasing in volume as the convulsion grew more intense.

And in that second, it happened.

His brain was so nearly mush that he almost missed it, but at the height of his body's arc, as his arms thrashed, he felt the restraints give.

Time seemed to stop.

That can't have happened. You must have imagined it.

He felt the restraints give a second time. His mind scrambled to make sense of it. They must not have anticipated the increased strength his body's convulsions would generate.

Time resumed and then sped up as he realized what this meant. *This is your chance!* His pain spurred him on, giving him inhuman strength, and he gathered it into the core of his being. Bellowing with all of his might he flexed his biceps and *pulled.* The groan of straining metal brought the Tormentor's head up from his clipboard.

"Good God," screeched the Tormentor, vaulting to his feet. "Put him out, man!" he yelled at the orderly. "Put him out!" The orderly scrambled toward the tray, trying to fill a syringe with sedative while the Tormentor whirled to the door. "Guards! Get in here!" They both snapped to order. One hastily keyed the code into the door, and the other removed the gun from his holster.

The Tormentor swung back around just as Eli overpowered the restraints with a primal yell. He held the Tormentor's alarmed gaze as the orderly approached from behind with the sedative. Without looking, Eli grabbed the orderly by his throat and wrenched him around to hold against his chest. Eli tore the syringe from the orderly's grasp and stabbed it into the man's jugular. As Eli growled low in his chest, never breaking eye contact with the Tormentor, his thumb depressed the plunger. The orderly sank to the floor.

With one hand he reached for the restraints at his ankles, keeping an eye on the guards at the door. The door hissed, and the guard with the gun rushed into the room, aiming at Eli's chest. With only one leg free, Eli grabbed the Tormentor to use as a human shield just as the guard pulled the trigger. The Tormentor's body jerked in his hands, and he heard the guard swear and fumble to reload his gun as the other guard pulled his own weapon.

Reload?

Tranq gun. They were shooting tranquilizers. Eli dropped the Tormentor and gazed in wonder at the bright floral marker of a tranquilizing dart protruding from his shield's chest.

Jesus, I might actually make it out of here!

Eli reached for his other ankle restraint as the guard who had already fired yelled, "Don't waste your shot! Make sure you can hit him or we're fucked!"

"You already are," Eli informed them as he moved to a crouch on the stretcher and waited for one of the idiots to take a shot. He knew he was due for another convulsion any moment, and it could be his last. He had to get far away from here so he could find someplace safe to die.

It took only a second before the guard to the left decided to take a shot, and Eli leapt to the side as the tranquilizing dart sailed past. Eli reached him in three strides and wrapped his arm around the guard's head. A quick twist and the satisfying crack seemed to freeze the remaining guard in horror.

The dead guard's body fell to the floor with a muffled thud. Eli crooked his finger at the other guard who now knew, with absolute certainty, that he was dead.

"P-please," the guard stuttered. "I never did anything to you!"

Eli lifted the corner of his lips in a cruel smile. "You're right." He stalked closer. "You're worse." He stopped right in front of the guard and snarled, "You. Watched."

Eli sprang forward, punching the guard in the throat hard enough to crush his larynx. The sick voyeur would never draw breath again.

Eli didn't stay to watch the guard drop to his knees and struggle in vain for breath. He felt the beginning twinges of another convulsion and knew he was out of time. Outside and to the right of the lab a staircase rose, ending in a solid wall.

Eli didn't understand this, but, with no other exit, began to climb. He only made it halfway up before the convulsion was on him. His muscles spasmed, throwing him forward onto the stairs.

Don't give up! You'll never get this chance again!

He shrieked as the spasms threw him from his front to his back. His spine ground into the edge of the stairs, ratcheting the pain to new levels.

Move, damn it! His mind and body were screaming, and he used all of that energy to roll himself over again.

He was able to pull himself to his hands and knees. With strength he did not know he possessed, he crept up the remaining stairs until he reached the top. His forehead bumped the wall that topped the stairs and, because he had no other choice, he stopped.

He banged his head in frustration against the only remaining barrier to his freedom and was shocked as it gave way. The entire wall began to swing away from him, revealing a room filled with medical equipment.

A false wall. Leading into a...*supply closet?* His strength was at its end, and his vision flickered and then went black. The poison had robbed him of his sight, one of the markings of the end.

It's over. He hadn't made it, and he would never get free now. Well, he'd be damned if he died one more time in that fucking room.

Moving by feel alone, he dragged his body over the threshold and into the closet. His legs were useless, and the numbness was creeping up his thighs toward his torso. The absence of feeling was a relief as it meant the end to at least some of his pain.

He heard the wall swing back into place and shuddered as it clicked shut. To finally die alone, even if he would awaken shackled to a stretcher again, filled him with peace.

He drew in what he knew was to be his last breath and jolted at what his brain latched on to. Peanut butter and jelly. The warm, yeasty smell of bread and the earthy aroma of chocolate. And . . . *woman?*

Fresh sunlight mixed with fabric softener and another scent that he couldn't quite place, but knew was unique to just *her.*

His body revolted, trying in vain to reject the death that was only a moment away. He had to live. He had to fight.

She was his, and she was in trouble. She needed him, but even beyond that—

I need her.

His heart stopped beating.

***

Abilene stared in bemusement at the retreating taillights.

"Bye, suckah!" Olive crowed from the backseat window as the car jumped the curb in its haste to be gone. Abilene shook her head. Sometimes, they really were just a bunch of kids.

She twisted the hem of her *Princess Bride* T-shirt and pondered, one more time, the pressing feeling she had that she was *supposed* to be here right now. She turned toward the hospital entrance.

Common sense dictated she should be in that car right now, headed toward an afternoon of napping and old *Dexter* episodes. Instead, she was here "to run labs" if she believed the excuse she'd given her co-workers.

She didn't.

Her Converses squeaked as she stomped in frustration down the hallway. There was nothing she would do today that couldn't wait until tomorrow. They didn't exactly have deadlines here at the hospital God forgot.

She passed the supply closet. Stopped. Turned around.

An overwhelming feeling of loss bowled her over. She looked toward the ceiling as wetness seeped into her eyes. *Homesickness.* Though, that didn't feel quite right. This was much more intense. Much worse.

She shuffled to the door and leaned forward until her forehead was pressed against the wood. Her hand crept up to be placed at heart level. She *ached* to be on the other side of that door. Her labs could wait. She twisted the knob and pushed the door inward . . . it met resistance. Had something fallen from the shelves to block the door? She pushed harder, pressing her shoulder against the door. Whatever it was, it was freaking heavy. She glanced down to check if she could see the problem, only to light upon the curled fingers of a man's hand.

"Oh my God!" she breathed, renewing her struggle with the door in earnest. It edged forward, but she was able to get it open enough for her to squeeze through. She froze to the spot.

"Holy. . . " *naked man.* In her usual spot across from the supply shelves, sprawled on his abdomen, was *the* biggest man she'd ever seen. His face was pressed against the wall, his arm stretched forward as though reaching for something.

She was stunned as she took him in. He was flawless. Physical perfection. Muscle carved elegant lines through his body. Broad shoulders tapered down to narrow hips. His exquisite unclad backside snagged her gaze, and her lips parted in an inaudible, "Oh."

Heat transfused her cheeks, and she jerked her gaze to the wall. Talk about unprofessional. This man lay here in medical peril, and she was ogling him like the headliner in Thunder Down Under.

"Oh my God, I'm really sorry!" she blurted, struggling to keep her eyes away from that life-changing ass.

Jeez, you are such a lech, Abilene Lynn Miller. She straightened as she realized his body wasn't moving with the regular rise and fall of respiration.

It spurred her into action as nothing else could. She dropped to her knees by his side.

"Sir?" She placed her hand on his head of thick, mocha-colored hair. *Please respond. Please!*

No response.

"Oh, *shit,*" she muttered. "Okay," her brain scrambled for her next step. "Okay, *what?!*" she brought a trembling hand to her temple. *Think. Think!*

One of her few strengths in her chosen field was efficiency in an emergency, but she had lost her shit at the sight of this unconscious man. There was a reason doctors weren't allowed to treat family members, and this was it. But this man was an utter stranger to her.

No. He isn't.

She laid her hand on his massive shoulder and gave a tug in an attempt to roll him over. He barely budged. She used her other hand, heaved, and he turned over. It threw her off balance, and she caught herself with a hand to his chest. She pulled it back as though burned.

He had the face of an angel, his dark lashes lay in spikes against his high cheekbones.

He is yours. Save him.

She leaned forward, all hesitancy lost. "I will fix this," she promised. Her fingers went to his neck in search of a pulse. Nothing. He didn't have a pulse, and he wasn't breathing. She gripped his jaw and tilted his head back.

"You stay with me!" she ordered as she pried his mouth open, sweeping her finger over his tongue and the back of his throat in search of an obstruction. When she found none, she bent forward and covered his mouth with her own to puff air into his lungs.

She recoiled, spitting. The *taste*. His mouth was bitter.

"Someone *poisoned* you?!" she screeched. She had never felt so angry in her life. As though, without any compunction whatsoever, she could tear this person, who had dared to harm him, to shreds with her bare hands.

She suddenly worried that she *wouldn't* be able to fix this. He wasn't breathing, had no heartbeat, and had been *poisoned*. She had no idea how long he'd been without oxygen, but a little voice of doubt was already whispering a possibility she refused to believe: *He's dead.*

"No!" There was still one more thing she could try. She snatched the crash cart toward herself. She grabbed both paddles of the defibrillator with one hand and the gel with the other. She squeezed gel onto his left side and right pectoral, set the defibrillator at 200 joules, and placed the paddles.

She shocked him, and his body jerked under the paddles. She tossed them aside and felt for a pulse. When she found none, she set the defibrillator charge to 360 joules and began CPR for the two minutes she had to wait until she could shock him again.

She went through the motions of compressions and breaths as her brain skimmed through her med school knowledge. She had to admit that she could only shock him one more time. Just once more, and then she would have to—*call it.*

She halted compressions and grasped the paddles once more,

placed them, and checked to make sure the defibrillator was charged before shocking him.

His big body jerked once more, and she set aside the paddles to reach for his pulse.

Nothing.

She heard a whimper and was shocked to realize that she had made it as she grasped his wrist, checking for his pulse there.

His body was still. Cooling to the touch. Lifeless. *Dead.*

She clutched the arm she held between her breasts and began to rock back and forth, making a keening noise that frightened her. *Why do I feel as though I am the one who has died?*

"I'm sorry," she moaned, pressing a kiss to his palm. "I'm sorry, I'm sorry—" Tears gathered in her eyes and slipped out of her closed lids.

Minutes passed as she kept vigil, rocking, her sobs filling the tight space—

His arm *jerked.*

She looked at his face, and her heart kicked as he took a huge gulp of air. Several rattling breaths followed, and he began to panic, scissoring his legs and arms as though fleeing an unseen foe. She moved to shush him, to assure him that he was safe, when the hand she was holding clutched her shirt, pulling her forward with inhuman strength.

She face-planted in his chest and instantly moved to pull back, sure that physical contact with a stranger would only increase his panic.

But he stilled.

His breath left him in a sigh; the hand she wasn't holding moved to cup the back of her head, and he secured her face against his chest. His body shuddered in what she could only describe as . . . *relief?* Something warm filled her chest. "Shhh," she murmured, stroking his hand with her thumb. "You're okay. Everything is okay now." As she rubbed her cheek against his chest, she was surprised to realize that it was.

***

Something was different. Eli could sense it. It has started the same way it always did. The black void interrupted by a flash of light, a gasp of breath. Panic had followed, and he'd struggled, jerking his arms and legs, his hands grasping, one of them finding purchase and tugging something toward him.

And then, his world had slowed down. His left hand moving, fingers burying in the softest thing he had ever felt. His right hand was being stroked in gentling circles, and he lay still to better absorb the sensations.

He was supposed to be afraid, wasn't he? He struggled to remember, everything was so murky, but he was certain that in the past, at this point, he always felt *fear*.

A low, feminine voice was murmuring soothing sounds to him, and he relaxed completely. There was nothing to fear here. In fact, for the first time since he could remember, he felt complete. Fulfilled.

He extricated his right hand and swept his arm out to haul a warm bundle of curves to his side. He felt her stiffen, and then she relaxed against him. He brought his face to where his left hand was nestled and inhaled.

Sunshine.

Some distant memory pinged in his brain. He knew this smell. It was important to him, but why? His arm tightened.

She began to struggle again, and he rolled over her, pinning her movements with the weight of his body. She pushed against his chest, small sounds of distress escaping her lips, and he grabbed each wrist and hauled her arms over her head, burying his face in her neck and inhaling once again.

It's her. She's the One.

His eyes opened in shock, and he found himself staring at a delicate ear surrounded by blonde curls. He lifted his head.

Wide, frightened, unbelievably blue eyes met his searching gaze.

"A-are you going to hurt me?" she stuttered.

Hurt her? He could never hurt her. How could she not know that?

He shook his head in confusion. Panicked breaths puffed out of her parted lips and fanned across his neck.

"It's you," he said. Her eyes widened in question. "You're here," he whispered, awe lighting his face. His vision focused on her lips once again. All he could see, all his world was focused on, was her mouth. It was so lush. A full bottom lip. Fuller, sensuously curved upper lip. Straight, white teeth. The tip of her tongue darting out to lick her lips.

His groin tightened at the sight, and he groaned. He had to taste her. It was imperative. He began to lower his head, never breaking his focus on her lips.

His head snapped up, and he sniffed at the air.

Something was wrong.

A hand seized his ankle.

Chapter Four

Abilene's eyes widened in shock. He was going to . . .*kiss* her? She was equal parts titillated and horrified. This situation was outside of the normal care dictated by the Hippocratic oath.

His size had been much less daunting when he lay prone and unconscious on the floor. Now, pressed against her from knee to chest, his enormous weight pinning her to the floor, he was pretty damn scary.

Okay, *and* he was the most attractive man she had ever seen. The fact that he was naked rushed back in, and she bit her lip to keep from embarrassing herself with a moan.

His gaze narrowed further on her mouth, his head lowered, and her stomach fluttered. Just as his lips nearly brushed hers, he jerked his head up; he sniffed the air like an animal.

His body was wrenched down hers, his hands scrambled for purchase on the linoleum floor, and Abilene couldn't comprehend what she was seeing.

The wall of shelving she viewed each day had swung into the closet, revealing . . . *a hidden door?* Beyond, she could see the top of a blond head. The man's hand was wrapped around the ankle of her patient, and he was tugging.

Her patient drew his free leg back and kicked the blond head sharply, causing the unidentified man to drop his hold. She heard his gasp of pain.

The last half hour had held too many surprises for Abilene, and she feared she was not handling it well. She heard herself hyperventilating as her patient grasped her by the shoulders and pushed her into the wall, shielding her against the blond man with his own body.

"Shhh, you're okay," he muttered, an echo of her earlier assurances to him. "I won't let you get hurt." Yet, even as he promised her protection, he shook his head as though dizzy, and

Abilene was reminded that just twenty minutes ago, he had been dead.

Her mind halted. *Wait a minute.* He couldn't have been dead. People didn't come back to life after they died.

Her hyperventilating worsened, and the closet around her swirled. She looked at the blond man again.

"M-major Taylor?" she stammered, confused even more.

Her patient recoiled as though struck. His eyes snapped to her face and demanded explanation.

"My boss," she clarified.

His shoulders slumped. "No," he whispered. His eyes flooded with rage, and the bottom fell out of Abilene's stomach. "Then you'll pay first," he growled.

He launched to his feet, pulling her up with him, all prior tenderness evaporating like mist. He swung her to his front, pulling her back against his chest. One arm clenched her around the waist, the other snaked around her neck, tightening and cutting off her air. No longer was he shielding her with his body. She now stood between him and Major Taylor, who aimed a rather scary-looking gun right at her chest.

She watched Major Taylor's smirk fade into a frown. "No," he whispered. His gun hand fell to the floor with a clunk, and his eyes rolled back into his head. "Abilene." Her name slipped out of his lips as he fell unconscious, his face hitting the floor with an audible smack.

At the sound of Abilene's name on Major Taylor's lips, her patient's arms jerked, as though the reminder of their familiarity with each other was horrifying to him. The arm around her throat tightened even more, and black dots crowded her vision.

"Oh, yes," he laughed without humor, "you will pay."

Her world went black.

***

She was a part of it. Eli looked at the man who had ruined him forever and then at the unconscious woman who, for a few seconds, had made him feel hope. For the first time in years.

She was just like everyone else he'd ever encountered: a betrayer.

A part of him still refused to belief that this woman slumped in his arms had any connection to the Tormentor. It was too cruel. Just as he had found her, to discover this?

Found her? He frowned. What the hell was that supposed to mean? He hadn't been *searching* for her.

She's a stranger. She's nothing to you.

The Voice countered: *The One.*

He groaned as he heaved her dead weight onto his shoulder in a fireman's hold. To hell with that!

His eyes scanned the closet and lit upon a pile of scrubs. With one hand he grabbed a pair of pants and pulled them on, securing the woman's weight to his shoulder with his other hand pressed firmly to her backside. The pants were tight on his thighs, and the hems hit him just below his calves. He looked like some caveman-like character out of *Lil' Abner,* complete with woman over shoulder, but it could not be helped.

He strode to the prone form of Major Taylor—he could now call him by his true name—and kicked him in the face. He considered ending him right now, but his desire to see the Tormentor's fear as he realized Eli was going to kill him prevented him.

"I'm coming back for you, you son of a bitch," he promised, then walked through the closet door and out into the hall.

This could get tricky. Staff members were sure to walk the hallways, and the sight of a half-naked man toting an unconscious woman was going to raise some red flags.

He craned his neck to the side, his ears taking in all sounds, even those a normal human could not hear. He could hear the air circulating in the vents. A fly buzzing down the hall to his left. The refrigeration unit in the vending machine to his right kicking on.

Even water dripping in what he assumed was a bathroom on the floor above. He heard not one sound that would indicate human presence in the building.

He grimaced, unnerved. His enhanced hearing capabilities had not failed him in the eight years since he'd tasted that damned—

She stirred, moaning. He adjusted his load and steeled his nerves. He would just proceed as though trouble lurked around every corner; then his assessment of the facility being empty, right or wrong, mattered not.

He moved forward, scanning each door, finding only empty rooms on the other side of the little rectangular windows.

What kind of a research facility had no staff?

A front. That's what kind of operation would be devoid of patients and staff. This building was here to hide *him*.

He increased his pace, certain now that no one was here to stop his escape.

His cargo moved again, more conscious now. He tightened his grip.

"Let me go!"

He snorted. "How do we get out of here?"

She wriggled, causing him to have to readjust his grip.

"I'm not going anywhere with you!" She began to pound his back with her fists and aimed a kick at him. He grunted at the kick and dropped her to her feet. She staggered back and blinked up into his face.

He leaned forward. "You're coming with me. Now, you can come easily, or I can put you out. You decide."

She swayed where she stood. "Please," she whimpered. "Please, don't do this." One tear traced down her cheek. Her knees crumpled, and he caught her as she lost consciousness again.

His gut clenched. Her plea was identical to what the Tormentor had elicited from him over and over.

The Voice whispered again, *The One. Do not harm her.*

He gritted his teeth. One thing was for certain: her involvement in his repeated torture deserved punishment. And he was going to mete it out.

He spotted the front exit.

He made the choice for Abilene. "We're outta here."

***

Abilene became aware of the constant hum of a car's engine. Before she could utter a sound, she began to remember. Saving a stranger who did not feel like a stranger. His miraculous recovery. His weight on top of her. His head lowering to brush his lips against hers.

She shivered. *Delicious.*

She stiffened, remembering what had come after.

Sick fear made her sit up straight. The man who had abducted her was watching her out of the corner of his eye. "Who are you?" she blurted.

"You know who I am." His tone was scathing. "You probably know more about me than I know about myself."

"I think there must be some mistake," she began. "Who exactly do you think *I* am?"

"Not gonna work, Abilene," he gritted, using her name like a blow.

"How do you—"

He cut her off. "I heard *him* say it, remember?" The car bounced as he pulled off onto a side road, then onto the shoulder. The bouncing intensified as he pulled behind a screen of bushes. He stopped the car. "Just after you admitted to me that he is your boss." He looked at her as though he were waiting for her to confess to something.

She shrugged, at a loss. "I'm sorry. I don't understand—I don't even know what you were doing there—"

He got out of the car, slamming the door behind him. He came around to her side, opened her door, and offered her a hand out. She stared at it in bemusement, and he jerked it behind his back, a look of chagrin crossing his face. Without saying a word, he turned on his heel and moved to the bushes, twisting branches off and gathering them into his arms.

What the hell was that? Manners?

She got out of the car on her own power and scanned their location, seeing a tight cluster of houses about half a mile away.

He seemed to pluck the thought from her head. "Don't even try it." He spoke without turning to look at her, continuing to collect branches as he walked. "I'll catch you before you make it a hundred feet."

He returned to the car with his arms full, and began placing the branches around the vehicle. Right before her eyes the car seemed to melt into the landscape. She gulped. If she had to be kidnapped, she much preferred an inexperienced idiot, not G.I. Joe.

He finished his blind, then moved to her, grabbing her hand and setting off in the direction of the houses. She dug in her heels.

"Where are we going?"

"Home."

Chapter Five

After grabbing her hand, her kidnapper had dragged her through a neighborhood that had fallen prey to foreclosures—no-trespassing signs dotting every window—before picking this dilapidated home in the middle of a cul-de-sac. Now, they sat in awkward silence against opposite walls of an empty, but filthy, living room as the setting sun leaked light. The man was getting antsier by the second, his gaze growing sharper and more uncomfortable.

Abilene tore her eyes from his to survey the room, noting with distaste the evidence that an animal had made, and then abandoned, a nest in one of the corners. She couldn't prevent a shudder. It was bad enough that she'd passed out twice in front of him today, but in a very short time—Abilene eyed the sun's shadows—it was going to be dark in here. He was bound to hear her sobs and notice that she was curled in a fetal position. People rarely missed that.

She had to break the silence. "What's your na—"

"How about a bedtime story?" he demanded.

"Um—" she faltered. "Okay?"

"You tell it."

She swallowed, apprehension tickling the back of her throat.

"In fact," he continued, "I have a request." He tapped his chin in pretend contemplation. "Oh yes," he looked at her again. "The Garden of Eden."

She jerked her head back at the unexpected words. "A *Bible* story?" Oh God, was he some kind of religious zealot?

That muscle in his jaw ticked again. "I'll even get you started," he paused. "Once upon a time . . . ."

Her mind knotted. She wasn't even sure she remembered any stories having to do with the Garden of Eden. And she was pretty sure she had never heard a Bible story begin with *Once upon a time*. He cleared his throat, his glare hostile. Ignoring his bizarre request was not an option right now.

"O-once upon a time," she paused, rubbing her damp palms against her jeans. She started again, "Once upon a time, Adam and Eve lived in the Garden of Eden." She shot him a glance. He waved her on impatiently.

Okay, so far, so good. She scanned her mind for what came next. "Um, they had a lot of pets and got all of their food from an apple tree?" The inflection of her voice rose at the end, turning her latest statement into a question. She winced.

He snorted. "How many apple trees you ever seen in a desert?"

Desert? Any picture books she'd ever seen had always shown the Garden of Eden as a lush, green paradise.

"I don't know the story!" she retorted. Chills were creeping up her arms, leaving goose bumps in their wake. Her mind was whispering at her to pay attention. That this was important—to them both. She took a shaky breath and looked at him from the corners of her eyes.

His face was a mask of anger. "Try again. There were two trees. What were their names?"

A spark fired in her mind. Okay, yes. She remembered this part. She could appease him and maybe bring down the intensity. "In the garden were two trees. The Tree of Eternal Life. . . ." The other's name was just out of reach— "And the Tree of Good and Evil," she finished in a rush. She looked at him, again, unsure of what his reaction would be, praying it wouldn't be violence. Why this story was affecting him so much, she didn't know, but she sensed she should tread cautiously.

He grunted. "Close 'nough." He waved her on. She hesitated. He sighed. "These trees came with rules, yeah? What were they?"

She frowned. His intensity had *increased*. He was getting more and more aggravated as the story progressed. She couldn't help feeling she was one slip-up away from retribution. But, retribution for *what?*

He clapped his hands once to get her attention again. "They could eat from the Tree of Life as long as—"

"I don't *know*—" *Oh God, please don't hurt me.*

He growled in frustration, his hand swiping the air to erase her words, "As long as they promised not to—" A beat of silence. He snapped his fingers at her.

She jumped. "Not to eat from the Tree of Good and Evil." He leaned forward in a crouch, for all the world looking as though he were prepared to spring.

"And what did the Tree of Life *do*, Abilene?" His voice had gotten quiet. Low. It was so much worse than screaming in her face, and she was afraid of him. She drew her knees to her chest and wrapped her arms around them.

"M-made them live f-forever," she stammered, flinching at the fear in her tone. Her voice was so soft there was no chance he had heard it from his spot across the room, but his body relaxed in response to her words, fight seeming to drain out of him in a rush.

He leaned his head back, and it hit the wall with a thud. She could see his Adam's apple bob up and down as he struggled to control his emotions. She refused to look away from him, waiting for what he would do next. Would he fly across the room and hit her? Break down and cry? Scream in rage?

He shoved a hand through his hair and exhaled. Looking at her with baleful eyes he spoke without tone. "Go to sleep. It'll be dark soon."

She watched as he stretched out on the floor and draped one arm over his eyes. His chest continued to rise and fall with his shuddering breaths.

He's not well. Her hand rose to her throat, and she could feel her heartbeat fluttering beneath her fingers. She looked to the window as the sun sank below the horizon.

She had to get away from him. The last few minutes had confirmed that beyond a shadow of a doubt. Even now, she could see him struggling to regain control, and she knew the only reason she wasn't dead right now was simple luck of the draw.

She had seen murder in his eyes, and she had been the target.

***

That had not gone as he'd hoped. As he'd *planned*. Eli lay on the floor with the coolness of his forearm pressed to his eyes. He was so sure he'd been about to trip her up. No ordinary person could have made it through that story without revealing what they knew. That is, if they *knew* anything to start with.

Doubt aimed at himself, crept through him like a plague.

What if you're wrong about her, it whispered to him. Oh *God*, how he wanted to be wrong. He needed her to be innocent of the crimes he suspected. Crimes against his own body. His soul.

Even with the need for vengeance roiling through him since learning of Abilene's connection to the Tormentor, he'd been beating back an insatiable hunger for her as a woman. As a lover. Even, God help him, as a friend.

Eli *liked* her. His time in the car with her had revealed glimpses of the type of personality he'd always gone weak in the knees for when he had been younger—and free. Growing up as he had in the South, he'd been surrounded by strong, sassy women, and this tiny, angelic-looking creature would have been able to hold her own against any of them.

He knew he scared her; he'd seen fear flash across her expressive eyes several times today. But more than once when that had happened, she'd belted him one. A verbal check that only helped along the admiration he was fighting back as though his life depended on it.

And his life may very well depend on it. He'd been lulled into a sense of trust before. The Tormentor had talked to him often in the beginning. Assured him that he was helping his country. That the information they were getting from the experiments could save lives, could mean the difference between winning and losing the stalemate in the Middle East.

That he would do anything in his power to make sure Eli's pain was minimal. Necessary.

Eli snorted. The death of that trust had been more painful than the physical deaths that had wrought it. That Eli had allowed himself to trust, even knowing trust only led to betrayal, was something Eli would never forgive himself for.

Or repeat.

He heard a noise from Abilene's side of the room. It sounded like she was fighting against the urge to cry.

Know the feeling, he thought, as he felt his anger at her soften even more. He resisted as long as he could.

He cleared his throat. "Abilene?She gasped, and he could hear her struggle to become even quieter. She didn't want him to know she was upset. Against his will, that admiration he'd been fighting warmed his chest.

"What's wrong?" he whispered, immediately cringing. *What's wrong?* Besides being attacked at gunpoint, being kidnapped, and then being held hostage by a stranger who demanded cryptic bedtime stories?

Guilt joined the admiration.

Oh, great. That's just. . .great. He sighed and began to crawl over to her tiny, shadowed form. He huddled over her, careful not to touch her in any way.

"Hey—" he began. What was he doing? Was he going to comfort her? That would be counterproductive. And if he were in her shoes—which he had been—he wouldn't accept comfort from his captor anyway. He was at a loss.

"It's s-so dark," she moaned, curling tighter.

His nostrils flared. *She's afraid of the dark?* He eyed her incredulously. *Well, that's. . . disarming.*

Damn it, it was fucking endearing was what it was. A force

inside him fought to offer her protection, to reward her instead of punish her for revealing this weakness to him.

"Okay," he wracked his brain for a way to accomplish that without alarming her further. "It's okay." Maybe she would feel better if she knew she wasn't alone? He moved closer to her to sit cross-legged at her back. He edged forward until his knee grazed her spine.

She stiffened, and he cursed, moving away at once. *You're an idiot*, he told himself. The last thing she would want to be reminded of in the dark was that *he* was there.

But once his knee was no longer in contact, she gasped and clutched at him over her shoulder.

"No!" she cried. "It's better." She shuddered and continued in a wavering voice. "It was better for that second."

He inhaled, completely out of his element. This was powerful stuff. That what he was offering was *working*, that he had made it better, even for a second—he exhaled and edged forward again.

When he made contact with her once more, she breathed out her relief and edged even closer to him until his thigh was pressed flush against her back. His breath caught in his throat.

"Eli," he whispered.

She stiffened.

"My name is Eli."

She breathed his name from between parted lips, and Eli felt his heart skip a beat, then quickly make up time.

Holy God, she was . . . *consuming*. He couldn't look away from her now-relaxed face and moonlit curls.

"Sleep," he murmured to her. "I'll make sure you stay safe."

She curled her hands beneath her chin in answer. He stared in rapt attention as her breathing slowed.

And he was still guarding her when she slipped deeply into slumber.

Chapter Six

Abilene was delectably warm and cozy. She hummed in satisfaction and snuggled deeper into the source of heat at her back. She couldn't remember the last time she'd felt this rested. This *secure.*

Complete awareness still hovered outside of her mind's reach, but she felt as though this moment was incongruous with what the situation called for.

She mentally shrugged. *Enjoy it. It's too good to pass up.* She sighed.

An answering and very male sigh sounded right behind her ear. She froze.

Her mind, sounding much too like her mother, screamed, *Oh my God, Abilene, what have you done?*

She was in *bed* with someone? She'd never, in all of her life, been in bed with a man, and that she was now was disconcerting, especially since she couldn't remember how she got here.

No, not in bed. The surface beneath her left hip was hard. Unyielding. It felt suspiciously like a floor.

She clenched her eyes tighter, forced herself to calm down, and began to take stock. A man's arm was curled beneath her cheek as a pillow. A firm thigh was nudged between her own. An arm curved over her side; a hand possessively cupped her breast. Something hard prodded her lower back and warm breaths puffed in her hair, ruffling her curls.

She wasn't just with a man as she'd first thought. She was *surrounded* by one. He invaded her space completely.

Eli.

Everything rushed back in, and she began to extricate herself.

At her first movement, Eli's arm tightened in reflex, urging her closer. He burrowed his face in her hair and rocked his hips, gently thrusting against her. Her eyes flew open, and she pushed herself away from him.

"Whoa!" His morning voice was gravelly and deep. He watched as she scrambled back and jerked to her feet, eyeing him suspiciously. She pressed her back against the wall, trying to get as far from him as possible.

He turned from her slightly and raised a knee, shielding his erection from her view as he rubbed his face and shook his head as if to clear the cobwebs. Her mouth went dry with conflicting emotions, remembering the exciting feel of him against her, the terrible rage in his eyes last night.

"Uhh...I must have fallen asleep." He brought his eyes up to a point over Abilene's shoulder. "It must have been scary waking up like that—" He broke off with an embarrassed grimace, then tried again. "After yesterday . . . I mean—Aw, hell." He shoved his hand through his hair and rose to his feet. "I would *never* hurt a woman like that. You don't have to fear that. Ever. That's not what this," he gestured between them while taking several steps toward her, "is about."

Abilene shrank farther into the wall. "Then what *is* this about?" she asked with as much grit as she could muster.

He stopped before her. "This is about making you pay for what you've done." The words were low and dangerous and teleported Abilene straight back to the previous night when Eli was all coiled strength ready to strike.

This morning, however, her nerves were shot, and her body was tightly wound from her alarming wake-up call. She could no longer play the wilting flower. "I've done nothing to you!" she shouted into his face.

She may as well have slapped him. He flinched, then charged her, closing the gap between them in one giant stride. He crowded her against the wall and placed two fists on either side of her face. "You will not lie to me," he growled.

Oh, God. She'd pulled the damn tiger's tail. She squeezed her eyes shut, and her hands flew to his chest to push him away, but he didn't budge. "I'm sorry," she whispered.

The muscles below her palms shivered, and her eyes flew back to his face.

Unidentifiable emotion raged in his eyes, but Abilene was almost positive that it was no longer anger.

"Don't touch me." His voice shook, and Abilene jerked her hands back as blood flooded her cheeks.

"I wasn't—I…."

A slight tremor shook his shoulders, and Abilene's words drifted off. Her palms burned from their contact with his body, and she curled her hands, trying to ignore the sensation.

"I can still feel your hands." He swore. "I can still feel your body from when we woke up."

Abilene licked her lips, and his gaze zeroed in on the movement. His brows drew together. He made a noise of distress.

"I'm sorry for what I'm about to do," he whispered just before his lips settled over hers.

Chapter Seven

His kiss was brutal. A punishment. Their teeth clashed together, and he pressed Abilene more firmly against the wall as he ground every inch of his tensed body into hers.

His lips were a brand; tingles spread like fire throughout her. She gasped, caught off guard, and he plunged his tongue into her mouth, invading her.

It was the most wonderful thing she'd ever felt.

Her tension drained in a flash, and she leaned into him with a plaintive moan. His flat blue eyes were sparking. A flush painted his cheeks, and his lips were parted. Harried breaths caressed her kiss-moistened lips. She'd never seen the face of a man lost in passion, but every feminine instinct she possessed was screaming at her that he was utterly lost—in *her*.

His erection prodded her belly. At the thought of that part of his body hard and unforgiving, something primal swept through her.

He is yours. Her lust exploded in response.

He's the One. Show him. Allow him to show you.

Show him. The directive caused an ache to settle low in her belly, a rush of moisture to pool between her legs. *Yes.* She needed to show him—in the most basic of ways—that she was his. She groaned at the intoxicating thought. Oh God, that he was *hers*.

His body responded to her groan, hardening even more, and she couldn't prevent an inexperienced squirm against him. He immediately rocked his hips into hers, then he bit off a curse as though he were trying desperately not to do it again.

But Abilene was already moving against him, wanting more. His firm thrust had been *magnificent*. She was dying for him to do it again.

"*Eli*," she pleaded, rubbing her face against his arm where it stretched by her head to clasp her wrists.

He hissed in a breath. "God . . . Abilene." His brows drew together. "You *want* this?"

Want. Oh, she most certainly *wanted.* Her entire body, her *existence*, was flooded with the feeling. If he didn't do something soon, she would unravel at the seams.

In frustration, she nipped at his arm with her teeth. *"Please."* She punctuated the whispered entreaty with another frenzied movement of her hips.

The groan that tore from his lips was long and low. "Holy God." He dropped her wrists to grasp her face with both hands, tipping her head far back until all she could see was his enthralled expression. Eli's vivid eyes held her gaze. *"Look* at you."

His thumb stroked the seam of her lips, and she parted them in response. Her tongue darted out to taste the saltiness of his skin. Her eyes slid shut in bliss.

He grunted as though in pain. *"Abilene . . . ."* He pushed his thumb further between her lips, and something wicked inside her urged her to suckle it. He swallowed noisily, and she could feel him hold his breath.

"Baby, let me kiss you again." His voice was fervent. Worshipful. "I won't take it any farther, but . . .please. I've got to taste you."

Her body thrummed. Her hands fisted in his shirt, pulling him forward. It was all the invitation he needed.

His lips settled over hers, the brutal anger of earlier absent from his every movement. Instead, she could feel him humming with intent and controlled hunger.

His tongue brushed her lower lip, asking permission this time before demanding entrance. She opened for him, and his tongue swept over her teeth, rubbing her own tongue in slow, sensuous caresses.

This was nothing like the awkward, pawing interactions Abilene had experienced in the past. Eli was an exquisite kisser. His every movement caused her gut to tighten, her fists to clench harder in his shirt.

49

She followed his lead and gently sucked on his tongue, and she knew his control had slipped as he groaned harshly into her mouth. His hands fell from her face. One arm wound around her lower back, hauling her against him. The other hand tunneled through her hair, cupping the back of her head to hold her still for a new onslaught of kisses.

She was no longer pressed against the wall, but held in his arms. Her weight straddled his firm thigh. The increased pressure at the apex of her thighs sent mouth-watering sensations bounding through her. She gave an experimental rock back and forth and was shocked when she cried out from the pleasure.

He growled in encouragement. "*Yes.* Oh . . .Abilene . . .*God.* Use me." His hand fell heavily to her ass, cupping her and urging her body to repeat the rocking movement. Her head fell back in awe, and she moaned in abandon.

As he rocked his own hips into her, he muttered a low curse and bit at her lips "I promised I wouldn't take it further, but you sound like you could. . . " he stopped to groan as she made another passionate noise, ". . . *come* from this."

His words shocked her, even frightened her. The situation had spiraled out of control, and she didn't know if she should pull away or grind harder into the flexing muscles of his leg.

Then his mouth was on hers once more, but this kiss was different. Instead of languid strokes, Eli thrust his tongue in and out of her mouth, mimicking the pace she was setting with her hips, and she knew she wouldn't be able to pull away from him, now or ever.

Her now-constant groan rent the air, and it got louder and louder with each of the writhing movements she made against him. Eli was making rough, primitive noises low in his throat as he ground his erection into her belly.

His demanding handling of her was causing a spring to wind tighter and tighter inside her. She was a doctor; she knew what was coming. What was barreling toward her like a freight train. And, damn, she couldn't wait to experience it. For him to experience it with her.

His hand slid from her hair to drift over her shoulder and collarbone. When she sensed its direction, she arched into him, thrusting her breast into his seeking hand. He snatched his lips from hers to gaze into her eyes. His look held challenge as he deliberately pinched her nipple.

And it was over.

Her orgasm flooded through her, throwing her head back with its force. She cried out loud and long, her hands twisting his shirt as she pulled him to her, needing to be as near to him as she could possibly be.

"*Abilene*," he groaned, burying his face in her neck and squeezing her even closer. He thrust roughly against her one more time and then shuddered as he began to come with her. She could feel wave after wave of pleasure roll through him as he moaned into the moist skin of her neck, biting her gently and then licking away the sting.

When the violent tremors of her release began to abate, she sagged, boneless in his arms, feeling completely sated. Secure in a way that frightened her.

She drew her head back and looked at him, her eyes filling with trepidation and humiliation as she realized what she had just done—and whom she had done it with.

He wore a shell-shocked expression, but as he reached out a still-shaking hand to brush a curl from her forehead, his eyes filled with a warm light. "God, you're beautiful," he whispered.

She burst into tears.

***

Eli stepped back, dropping his hands from her and trying to appear as non-threatening as possible. Any afterglow faded into the wall.

Abilene curled in on herself, crossed her arms over her front in a self-hug, and just cried. Big tears rolled down her cheeks; wracking sobs shook her slight frame.

This was not good. He hadn't had a ton of encounters with women, but he'd never gotten this reaction after sex.

His head snapped up. *Holy shit.* They hadn't even gotten to the actual sex part. He hadn't touched her bare skin or seen her lush naked body, and he'd come harder than he had in any of his other full-blown, no-holds-barred experiences.

He'd come inside his pants like some idiot high school kid. Eli's cheeks flamed with embarrassment. His only consolation was that it had been unavoidable. The moment their lips had touched, the pleasure had been too great, her wanton responses too stimulating. Hell, he'd do it again in a heartbeat, embarrassment or not.

Abilene's sobs pulled him back to reality. His gut clenched at the sight of her anguished face. He *felt* her pain. His stomach hurt for her, and he was compelled to slay her dragons.

Unfortunately, the smart man's gamble said that Abilene's dragons right now were none other than Eli himself. And so, not only did he feel like he wanted to cry with and for her, but he was appalled with his actions. *Ashamed* of himself.

He lifted a hand to brush her shoulder or touch her hair—he wasn't sure which—but he caught himself and let his arm fall back to his side. He cursed.

"Ah, Abilene—" He shoved a hand through his hair. "I'm sorry." He fought himself with all of his strength to keep from touching her again. She looked so forlorn and small. "Please—don't cry. Yell at me; hit me, if you want to. God knows I deserve it."

She raised flooded eyes to his face, multiple emotions roiling warring with each other. "I-it was just so wonderful . . . and you're s-so," she hiccuped as she searched for a word, "*horrible.*"

She was right. He'd just gotten done promising her he would never hurt her this way, and then he'd done it.

"Why? Why would you do that? You don't even *like* me." she whispered.

His shoulders slumped. He shook his head, disgusted with himself for so many reasons, the main one being he *shouldn't* like her. He wasn't sure that was the case.

"Okay, we need to hash a few things out," he finally muttered as he gestured for her to take a seat on the floor. *No more dancing around.* His fishing last night had gotten him nowhere. It was time to come out with it.

Abilene slid down the wall and clutched her knees to her chest. Eli took several steps back to give her space, then slowly sank to the floor himself, trying to look as unintimidating as possible.

"Last night you asked me what I was doing in your hospital," he began.

***

Abilene tilted her head. She wasn't sure she was ready for serious conversation, but this sounded promising. Maybe she would finally find out why he had taken her. "That's right—*my* hospital. I work there."

He seemed to consider this a moment, and then, "Well, you must have worked there a long time, then."

She sighed. "Three weeks," she mumbled. She clutched her knees closer to her body, hoping to still the tremors that were still racing through her limbs.

He sucked in a breath. His expression was . . . *relieved?* She frowned.

"That long, huh?" he asked quietly.

She felt compelled to explain. For some reason, she couldn't stand the idea that he would think her incompetent or unprofessional, and the rest was sure to come out at some point, anyway. "I'm a real doctor. I just . . .uh . . . haven't been one for very long."

"How long?" His question was urgent.

She brought her eyes to his and hesitated at their intensity. "Three weeks," she whispered.

Something in his eyes flickered. "You're not lying to me?"

Abilene's frustration crowded back in, obscuring her embarrassment. "Yes, Eli, I'm lying to you. When asked about my professional experience, I *lied* by picking the most unimpressive span of time imaginable."

All of his air left him in a whoosh. "That's...not what I expected." He closed his eyes and seemed to draw into himself.

Abilene waited several minutes for him to continue before she couldn't wait anymore. "Now that we've established what I was doing there. What were *you* doing there?" She straightened as she remembered another detail. "And why in hell had you been poisoned?"

His eyelids rose as though made of lead, and he stared at her for several heartbeats. Just when she was sure he would never answer her, he said, "What I was doing in the facility? Abilene, I was a prisoner in that building. I've been a prisoner for eight years. And I was *sure*," he spat the word, "that you were involved in keeping me there."

She blinked. "A...." *prisoner*? Unbidden, memories bombarded her mind: a hidden door behind the shelving, a medical facility without patients, suspicious drills.

Poison.

She shoved the memories aside, and took a deep breath. Okay, there was definitely something going on here, but to allege that he'd been in prison for eight years? The facility hadn't even been functioning for eight years. His story didn't ring true.

Then she remembered that the facility was slated to become a PTSD treatment center. Her pulse kicked.

He could be a patient. This could explain the drills. Were they bringing in PTSD patients under the cover of the drills to keep them secret for now? She evaluated Eli with a doctor's eye. To want to keep this man secret, he must have been involved in classified or black operations. There's no way they would let a recently graduated medical student have access to his treatment.

Unless I prove that I can cut it.

Her eyes roved over Eli again, now seeing in him the possibility of securing her future career. This was it—her opportunity. She would treat him for PTSD, return him to Needles, and snag a position at the top of the newly turned research facility.

Her stomach twisted at the memory of all of those days running labs. She could do this. She had to. "Okay, Eli, I'm listening," she told him, her voice smooth and professional.

His head snapped in her direction, his eyes narrowing in suspicion, and she mentally kicked herself. Her behavior could not drastically change; he would notice—as he just had—and distrust would stop the treatment before it began.She decided to change tactics. "Why did you think *I* was involved?"

Eli's eyes lost their light. "You said he was your boss."

He?

Puzzle pieces fell into place. Major Taylor. In Eli's mind, Major Taylor was some kind jailor keeping Eli at the facility against his will.

She had to make Eli feel like she was on *his* side, not Major Taylor's. "Well, I'm not involved. I didn't even know you were there, Eli. I would have done something if I had." *Like begin your treatment sooner.*

He nodded. "I believe you. I'm sorry."

She blinked at the grossly underwhelming olive branch. She had been through hell in the last twenty-four hours. Before she could stop it, the fuse on Abilene's temper went off. "You're *sorry?* For kidnapping me. You're sorry."

He nodded again. For the first time since this whole nightmare began, he looked properly shamed. *Unbelievable.*

"Well, since Hallmark doesn't make a card for that, I have a better idea for how you can apologize." She leaned forward. "Take. Me. Back."

He clicked his tongue. "See, here's the thing. You *are* involved. It may not be in the way I first suspected, but your presence in that building was *not* an accident. I can't let you go."

She bristled, ready to rip him a new one, but he wasn't done yet.

"Besides," he'd adopted that too-casual tone again, "something has been . . . whispering at me since the moment I sensed your presence in that closet." He eyed her. "It's been saying that you belong to me. That you're 'the One.'"

He ran his fingers through his hair. She waited with dread for the next shoe to drop.

"Abilene, even if I *wanted* let you go, I don't think I'd be able to."

***

"I'm not alone here, am I?" he whispered.

She shook her head once. "I-it said that? That I'm 'the One'?"

He nodded. "Sound familiar?"

"In the. . .I thought I heard—" She swallowed. "I've heard it, too." She paused.

"What does it mean?"

"Hell if I know," he said. His eyes narrowed on her.

She flinched. "It's not *my* fault!"

He glowered, angry all over again that she was invading his thoughts, taking over his senses. "You sure about that?"

Her grit returned in a flash. "Oh, this is just great! Yes, let's add this to the growing list of 'Ways Abilene is Ruining Eli's Life,'" she made air quotes with her fingers. "It starts with how I forced you to kidnap me, and ends, for the time being, with me somehow compelling you to keep me with you. I'm sure some new hardship will crop up momentarily, and then we can add *it* to the list, too."

Now he flinched. *Keep your cool, man. Play nice. Get her on your side.* She had a point. Well, he sure as hell wasn't going to admit *that.*

For some reason, she had believed him, or at least pretended to believe him, when he had told her he'd been a prisoner in the facility. He hadn't expected that. Apart from some initial doubt, she had swallowed his story whole.

Of course she believed you; you gave her the believable version of everything, the Voice scolded.

True. If he had told her the nature of the experiments. The reason why he couldn't die and *stay* dead. . . .

Well, suffice it to say, the outcome of their conversation would have been vastly different.

She opened her mouth to say something else, but a noise from outside brought Eli to full alert.

In less than a second, Eli had Abilene flat on the ground beneath him, covering her with as much of his body as possible. She struggled for breath, and he knew he'd knocked the wind out of her. He gazed down apologetically, and his gut wrenched when he noticed her blue eyes were filled with fear.

She gasped in a breath when her diaphragm unfroze, but Eli placed his fingers gently over her lips, shaking his head once and mouthing a silent *shhhh.*

Just then a clatter sounded from two houses down. Abilene's eyes grew wide, and she nodded to let him know she understood. He was embarrassed at how relieved he felt to see her fear vanish.

He bent down further and put his mouth directly against her ear. "We have to move," he breathed.

He didn't wait for her acknowledgment before scooping her up with him and pulling her toward the back door he'd scouted out the night before. He walked hunched over and noticed with approval that Abilene was following suite.

Eli didn't know if the noises from outside were from squatters or someone who meant Eli harm, but he wasn't going to wait around to find out. Whoever it was had already moved to the house right beside theirs.

Eli stuck his head out the back door and quickly ascertained that no one was in the backyards adjacent to this one. There was thick brush dead ahead, and Eli tugged Abilene toward it.

As soon as they were hidden among the foliage, a local policeman rounded the corner and entered the back yard, his gun held at the ready. Eli pulled Abilene farther into the brush just as the policeman noticed the house's open back door.

The man straightened and jerked out his walkie-talkie. "I think I've found them," he whispered into the device. "Send back-up!"

The walkie-talkie squawked once, and then Major Taylor's voice crackled through, "Hold your ground. Do *not* go in until I get there!"

Abilene stiffened beside him just as Eli's stomach dropped. The car. They had to have found the car.

"Damn it," Eli whispered. He wasn't free.

Yet.

Eli continued to pull Abilene through the brush until they reached another backyard. A quick visual scan told him there were no officers nearby, and he took off at a silent sprint, tugging Abilene behind him.

When they were out of hearing range, Abilene gasped out, "They came after you. With *guns!*"

The horror in her voice brought Eli to a skidding halt, but one look at her face, and he could tell she was appalled with the officers and Major Taylor, not with the fact that she had been abducted by someone who merited an armed man-search.

Progress.

"Yeah, I noticed that," he said with a quick smile. "We've gotta get out of here, darlin'. They're not going to stop once they find we've bugged out."

He scanned their surroundings. This neighborhood hadn't been struck as badly as the abandoned one. Signs of life dotted several of the houses and yards. A few houses over, Eli spotted wash out on the line that might actually fit him. He headed toward it, Abilene's hand still tucked inside his, and pulled a t-shirt and pair of jeans from the line. He didn't stop to put them on just yet, but continued to the street, remembering he'd seen a convenience store nearby when he'd been driving last night.

A few minutes later, Eli was punching out the window of the convenience store with his t-shirt-covered fist while Abilene glared at him.

"Do you have to break in?" she asked.

"They're not open," he said as he reached past the jagged glass and disengaged the lock. He opened the door wide for Abilene to proceed ahead of him. She sniffed at him, but then walked into the dark interior.

The door chimed behind him. "Why don't you find some breakfast while I change clothes?" he asked, reaching for the drawstring of his scrubs. Abilene spun away with a gasp.

"Okay," she whispered. He could tell she was blushing, even without being able to see her face, and grinned to himself.

She was fun to tease.

While Abilene roamed the aisles, he quickly pulled on the jeans and t-shirt. Both were a little tight on him, but they were way less-conspicuous than his ill-fitting scrubs and bare chest. He glanced at Abilene to make sure she wasn't watching before moving to the cash register. The cash drawer key winked at him in the light, and Eli shook his head at small-town life.

It's almost like home, he thought as he relieved the register of its cash, guilt nibbling at his conscience.

And just like that, Eli had a plan.

Home.

He had to go home.

He would never be free until Major Taylor was no longer a threat, and Eli knew of only one man who could make that happen: Sergeant Collins.

Eli glanced at the cash in his hand. Enough for a cross-country trip.

A feminine *ahem* caught his attention, and Eli looked up to find Abilene staring at his handful of ill-gotten gain.

"I'll pay it back," slipped out of his lips before he could stop it.

She didn't buy it, but she didn't tell him to put it back either, and he wondered again what part she had to play in all of this.

He couldn't very well let her go now; she could tell the authorities about him. And he would *not* pay attention to the warm feeling in his chest at the thought of taking her home to Georgia with him.

He couldn't afford any distractions.

But distraction or not, he really had no choice....

"We need to go to Georgia," he blurted out.

She raised both of her eyebrows and examined him for several long moments. Finally, "Okay."

Eli waited for the catch.

It didn't come.

"Okay?" he repeated.

She took a deep breath and brushed her curls back. "Look, something is going on here, and I want to know what it is. Besides that, I'm not going to fool myself into thinking I have a choice as to whether or not I go with you anyway. And you *will* let me go once we have everything figured out?" She paused.

He nodded dumbly, unsure of why this was going his way.

"Well, then...okay," she finished with a shrug.

They looked at each other.

She shifted her weight and raised an eyebrow. "Sooo...are we going to go or what?"

Eli forced himself to move, stomping out of the convenience store without waiting to see if Abilene followed.

She confused him at every turn. And for some reason, though he'd gotten his way, he felt like he had just lost a very important battle.

He mentally slapped his cheeks and avoided looking at Abilene's slight form where it had stopped beside him. It was time to act.

Step one: steal a car.

Chapter Eight

Abilene was the first to wake the next morning. She blinked in the early morning light and surveyed the dingy hotel room in whatever God-forsaken hole Eli had finally stopped in after twelve solid hours on the road.

This was officially the most awkward road trip of her existence. She had been ecstatic that he'd given her an excuse to stay with him yesterday. She needed to stay with him to make him better, and he did *not* belong back at the facility. They were coming after him with guns? She was a baby in the medical field, but even she knew that would set him back, perhaps permanently, if he was suffering from PTSD.

But now, she wasn't sure the possibility of heading up a medical facility was worth the torture of being strapped to the side of her silent, brooding patient for the amount of time it would take to make headway with him. He hadn't talked to her once, even when she'd tried to start conversation.

Granted, her conversation starters were pretty glaring diagnosis tactics....

Her eyes sought him out across the room. He lay flat on his back in the other double bed. He'd lost his shirt sometime in the night, and his bare chest gleamed as it rose and fell with his breathing.

Abilene's mouth went dry.

She was in trouble. Every time she looked at him, she had very unprofessional feelings. And, God, when he touched her, Abilene *burned.* Sensation after sensation plowed through her until mere kissing and touching were not enough. She wanted them naked. Straining.

Maybe she was lucky that her medical school schedule had kept her from dating. She would have gotten nothing done if she was this easily distracted by a handsome face and hard body.

Flawless body, her mind corrected.

Time to move, before he woke up and caught her staring at him and drooling. That would be hard to explain. She extricated herself from bed only to stub her toe on the night stand. She swore before she could stop herself. Her eyes flew to Eli. His breathing hitched, but he rolled to his side and continued sleeping.

She dared to brush the hair from his face. With his face relaxed, he looked *young*. Gone were all traces of the intensity he'd portrayed since she'd first seen him. He looked maybe 25 or 26. Her age, 27, at the most.

Funny, she would have sworn he was much older than that. He had a hardness to him that denoted experience and a tough life.

He sighed in his sleep and turned his face into her hand. She jerked it away.

When he made a contented noise and snuggled deeper into the pillow, she looked at the room again. Her eyes drifted to the open bathroom door, and a different kind of longing filled her.

Shower.

She gave a groan of pure anticipation and tripped over her own feet as she scrambled into the bathroom, closed the door, and leaned against it to eyeball the simple shower/bathtub combo with unadulterated lust.

"Hello, gorgeous. Where have you been all my life?" She tore her clothes off and reached beyond the shower curtain to turn on the water, flipping the dial to the hottest setting. She barely waited long enough for the water temperature to warm before snagging her panties from the clothes pile on the floor and hopping in.

Abilene drizzled shampoo on her underwear as makeshift laundry detergent, rinsed them, and then flung them over the shower curtain. She may have to put her dirty clothes back on after this shower, but a girl could face anything with a clean pair of chonies.

That chore handled, Abilene turned to the feeble spray, raising her face worshipfully. The water cascaded down her back, soothing her aching shoulders, scalding her skin clean.

Her skin began to tingle where the water hit her. She looked down at her body questioningly. *Well, that's new.* It was the strangest thing, but the tingles spread until they encompassed every square inch of her skin.

And it was *uncomfortable*.

Abilene reached through the curtain to grab the rough washcloth from the sink, and set to scrubbing her skin to get the irritant off. Her attempt didn't lessen the itching feeling. The only real result of the scrubbing was red, angry skin.

She shut off the water and exited the shower, her eyes taking in her dirty clothes pile with foreboding. Maybe she had picked up something in the road dust. Well, she would delay putting them back on as long as possible. Maybe it would give her skin a rest. She shook the clothes out over the bathtub, brushing them down with the damp washcloth.

Then she plucked the cheap hair dryer from its nest in the wall and set to drying her dripping panties. She'd gotten them down to the point of being damp when a knock on the bathroom startled her. She projected her voice through the door, "What's up?"

"Breakfast is served," Eli called through the door. "We need to hit the road soon, so be as quick as you can. I want a shower, too."

Images of Eli in the shower flowed through her mind before she could stop them, and she scratched another itch where it had cropped up behind her ear.

She gritted her teeth against the clammy feeling of her damp underwear as she pulled them up her legs. She pulled on the rest of her clothes, hoping to warm her underwear through incubation. She opened the door to find Eli sitting on his bed, bags from McDonald's spread around him, a sheepish smile on his face.

"I assumed breakfast at McDonald's held as much draw as supper," he offered. Abilene smiled at the gesture. She knew from his face last night when she'd requested the fast food chain that he was not a Ronald fan, and it warmed her that he would suffer through another greasy meal for her.

She ducked her head in acknowledgment of his guess and reached out to take the hot coffee he extended toward her. Another infernal itch protested from the back of her thigh, and she rubbed it through her jeans. She opened her mouth to ask him if he was experiencing similar rash-like symptoms—maybe they could figure out the problem by comparing notes—when she became aware that he was looking at her with an expression that resembled . . . *liking* her or something. His eyes were soft. He wore a half-smile. He wasn't being horrible.

Maybe it had been better when he was a jerk. His current expression was doing funny things to her insides. She thought back to yesterday. He hadn't been that angry man who'd snatched her from the supply closet since finding out she'd been a doctor for only three weeks, and therefore, not a participant in his imprisonment.

Which didn't mean he wasn't bat-shit crazy. She needed to sit down and have a serious talk with her libido. Something along the lines of *We will not be jumping the bones of anyone who kidnaps us, drags us to the Bible belt, and thinks he's Frankenstein's monster.*

He reached forward and wrapped one of her damp curls around his finger, then moved his hand from her hair to trail down the side of her face. She shivered and scratched her itching stomach. She pulled away from his touch and stepped back to put distance between them. It was one of the hardest things she'd ever done.

The uncomfortable itchy feeling spread to cover her whole body. She frowned and looked at Eli again, making a connection between him and the rash-like feeling that alarmed her.

His face grew bemused at her scrutiny. "Um, I'll go ahead and hop into the shower, okay?" He backed away carefully, and she wondered what she must look like to have him treating her so delicately. "Can we be ready to go in about five minutes?"

She nodded, her thoughts embroiled in her hypothesis. She didn't even notice when he closed himself into the bathroom. Her mind was flipping through case studies she'd gone through in her classes.

Case studies about addiction and withdrawal.

Smokers often exhibited a nervous, twitchy itchiness as they struggled not to smoke. She felt an itchy feeling when she longed for Eli. When Eli was near her. When she pulled from his touch.

Damn, damn, damn!

She was going through withdrawal. From Eli! Was she addicted to him? Her mind returned to the case studies. She'd never come across any studies concerning addiction to another person. It sounded far-fetched and unlikely. For her to become addicted to him, he would have to be producing something—a hormone or chemical—that could cause dependency. Pheromones were powerful, but she'd never heard of someone becoming addicted to them, despite what cologne commercials claimed.

Was Eli addicted to her, too?

The shower shut off and a moment later, he emerged from the steamy bathroom. The scent of clean man wafted to her, and she clenched her fists against the urge to scratch her neck.

His damp hair dripped onto the shoulders of his t-shirt, and the material of his clothes clung to the moisture on his body. She nearly groaned at the mouthwatering sight, but she remembered to look at his face, to check for any sort of sign he was being affected similarly.

The damn man looked cool as a cucumber.

Not fair.

"You ready?" When she nodded, Eli moved to the bedside table and pulled the drawer open. He made a small victorious sound, and then pulled the Gideon Bible from the drawer and closed it.

She looked at him, but he ignored the obvious question in her eyes. He collected the bags containing their breakfast and led the way out of the motel room. He marched to the truck he'd *stolen* yesterday—she was still miffed about that—went to the driver's side, and opened the door for her.

"You're driving," he said.

Her mouth worked like a fish. "Me?"

"Yup. I plan to lie down in the seat. Anyone looking will only see a woman, by herself." He smiled at her. "Go ahead. Fawn over my genius."

He looked so adorable with his wet, spiky hair and wide grin. Abilene moved her hand to her mouth, covering her smile. It just so happened that Abilene had no problem with this plan. She *loved* to drive.

"Works for me," she told him as she slipped past him and into the driver's seat.

He handed her the seatbelt, a look of mock-sorrow on his face. "Your fawning needs some serious work, darlin'."

He shut her door. Her eyes devoured his broad shoulders and flat stomach as he walked around the hood of the car to his side. He tossed open the door, hopped in, and slid across the bench seat quicker than her eyes could follow. Without any warning, he pulled her to him with a hand to her nape and pressed a firm kiss to her lips. His tongue plunged into her mouth, probing every inch in a few breathless seconds.

Just as always happened when Eli touched her, heat flashed through her entire body. She couldn't breathe, couldn't think, couldn't do anything but focus on where their lips met. She was about to beg him for more when he pulled away. "No eye-raping without consequences, darlin'." His breath was coming in short bursts, and Abilene could tell by the look in his eyes that the kiss had gotten away from him. He pulled himself away.

Abilene jumped when Eli stretched his body out on the seat

and placed his head in her lap. Her stomach dropped, and then coiled in desire. Parts of her body that she usually wasn't aware of were ordering her to pick up where the kiss left off. Her hands clenched the steering wheel. The itch became nearly unbearable.

"What are you doing?" she squealed.

He opened the Bible he'd taken from the motel room. "Research."

Research? She watched as he flipped through the Bible, stopped at a place toward the beginning, and began to read. She watched him for several moments before he tilted his head back to look up in her eyes.

"What's the hold up?"

"Um, nothing?" Her voice squeaked as she twisted the key. The engine turned over, and she pulled out of the motel parking lot and headed toward the freeway.

His piercing gaze stayed on her for a few more moments, his eyes telling her that he knew she was avoiding something, but then he turned back to his "research," and she focused on the road.

She rolled her head on her neck, straining not to scratch one of the many places that prickled with awareness due to Eli's close proximity.

Oh, lord.

It was going to be a long day.

Chapter Nine

Eli shut the Bible and rested it on his chest with a satisfied air. He'd found some answers, and it made him confident that they could figure this situation out. It seemed to be growing more and more . . . *intricate* each moment.

He was making the right decision in traveling home. Sergeant Collins would put a stop to this. There was no way Major Taylor had permission to do what he was doing. The risk alone to the government if he was found out....

No, Taylor had definitely gone rogue. And Collins had enough high-up connections to put the Tormentor away for the rest of his life.

He craned his head back on Abilene's thigh to look up into her face. She was refusing to look at him, which was just fine with him; it gave him a chance to observe her uninterrupted. It hadn't escaped his notice that she seemed twitchy today, scratching nervously whenever he was near.

He'd only noticed because he'd woken up in the same uncomfortable situation this morning. Well, not the *same* situation, exactly. Given what he'd observed in her throughout the car ride today, Eli had been much worse off this morning than Abilene was now.

He'd wakened fully erect, *needing* Abilene as he'd never merely wanted a woman before. And, God, his skin had been crawling. Not having her, then and there, had been a torture so severe it had rivaled all of the years Eli had spent in the lab.

Abilene had been in the bathroom taking a shower. The sounds of her splashing around had taken him to the point of physical pain. He'd resisted as long as he could, but within seconds, one of his hands had found its way into his jeans.

Red had crept up his neck and cheeks, embarrassment tightening his chest, but even the risk of Abilene coming out of the bathroom and finding him . . . taking matters into his own hands had not deterred him. In the end, getting caught was a nonexistent possibility, anyway. He'd lasted thirty seconds. Tops.

The relief he'd felt as he came had been so much more than physical gratification. The tingles that had been rippling over the surface of his skin faded into oblivion. He'd still wanted Abilene with an ache—his own hand was, after all, a very poor substitute for the petite blonde who made him stupid with lust—but being with her became an imperative that could be delayed a bit.

Now, just a few hours later, the tingles had already returned, causing him to lose his grip on the anger that kept him from her.

Abilene's lap was a luscious pillow. He felt surrounded by her, cocooned in her warmth, and he was enjoying every second.

Eli just resisted rubbing his face like a cat against Abilene's thigh. She'd been a tightly strung wire since he'd plopped his head in her lap this morning, and he wasn't ready to make her bolt. He wanted her to stay close.

It was time to face facts. Something almost . . . *supernatural* was occurring between them. Eli felt a biological compunction to be around Abilene. To protect her. To develop a relationship with her. To bury himself between her thighs.

And he *loved* it.

Abilene was incredible. He admired almost everything about her. She was funny. Smart. She put him in his place. She was sexy as hell.

Eli had no idea small, blonde women were his type. He'd always been interested in tall, stacked brunettes. But, damn, Abilene's sweet curves, her tiny stature, her blonde ringlets . . . they just did it for him.

Eli could tell they were both getting to the point where avoidance of one another was painful—emotionally and physically—and if peace needed to be made, Eli was going to have to be the one to make it. He had, after all, kidnapped the woman and held her against her will. Not the best first date.

They'd been on the road for a few hours, so he felt it was safe enough to sit up. Truth be told, he'd lain in Abilene's lap far longer than necessary.

When he straightened and moved over to the passenger side of the truck's cab, Abilene relaxed, although she did scratch at the spot on her thigh that had supported his head.

"So, how're you doing? You need a break? Want to switch?" Eli asked.

"I'm fine."

Eli squinted out the front windshield, searching for some indication of where they were. He'd been in his own little world since they'd set out, and she could have taken them to Canada for all he knew.

"Where are we?"

"Somewhere in Oklahoma."

Eli recognized their location and gestured to the approaching exit. "Take this one. I need to stretch my legs."

Chapter Ten

Abilene craned her head back. And back. She brought her right hand up to shield her eyes, and was finally able to make out the facial features of the twelve-foot tall statue of a Native American before her.

She flicked her eyes sideways and caught Eli's form in her peripheral vision. He was waiting for her to say something, bouncing around on the balls of his feet.

"Wow," she said. "That's really—" She paused to clear her throat. "He's really something." What else could she say? The statue was so far from politically correct it redefined boundaries.

Eli hadn't noticed her cautious tone, thank goodness, and bounced once more before settling back on his heels. "Isn't he? Trust me, he's even more impressive when you're nine."

"You've been here before?" Abilene asked.

Eli nodded. "When I was a kid…." He drifted off, then cleared his throat. "Come on, let's check out the trading post. We can get lunch." Eli walked back to her, grabbed her hand without ceremony, and tugged her toward the dilapidated shop behind the statue.

The smell of animal skins bowled her over as they strode into the trading post. She skidded to a stop. The trading post was filled with wall-to-wall souvenirs, each marked with a sign reading "Authentic." She smiled at Eli's obvious excitement. This trading post was no more "authentic" than Lucille Ball's trademark red hair.

He nudged her with his shoulder. "Go on. Look around." Where his shoulder had innocently touched her, she burned. Throughout the day, the tingles of this morning had morphed into something much more serious. Every contact ended in physical pain. It was not the contact itself that was painful; it was the withdrawal that nearly did her in.

This realization caused her to clutch at his hand when he dropped her own. He looked at her when he noticed as she grimaced against the uncomfortable sensations coursing through her.

"I'm fine," she assured him through gritted teeth. His expression said he didn't believe her, but he gave her some space anyway, walking away from her to look at some tomahawks. She exhaled in relief. It was just unfair that touch seemed to affect him so little.

She continued to watch him as he moved throughout the shop, finding more joy in observing his child-like reactions than she would find in her own window shopping. He had to trail his fingers over *everything* as he walked. Abilene found herself irrationally jealous of a pile of rabbit pelts, a box of arrowheads, a bow and arrow set. When she found herself envying a stuffed beaver, she knew it was time to snap out of it.

She walked over to a display of turquoise jewelry. She became enthralled with the depth and beauty of the stones as her thoughts turned inward.

Today, things were different. Eli was treating her differently. He'd always been polite and considerate, even when she'd been nothing but a kidnapping victim to him, but today, he was *kind.* She wasn't an idiot; she could tell he'd turned on the charm, but *why* he had decided to charm her was still a mystery. Abilene just hoped it wasn't for the sole purpose of getting into her pants, because, God help her, she could barely resist him as it was, even knowing she had to remain professional.

"Hey," Eli said at her shoulder, startling her from her revelry and causing her to jump. "Whoa, sorry," he offered as he casually brushed her lower back with the flat of his palm. He'd meant the gesture to be comforting, but as his hand dropped back to his side, Abilene couldn't prevent a groan as intense pinpricks bordering on torture swamped her.

The next second, Eli was in her face. "Are you in *pain?*" he asked, his voice intense. The force of the question took Abilene aback. "I'm fine," she whispered, finding it impossible to put enough emotion behind her words to convince him. "I'm just going to go use the restroom. Meet you back in the truck?"

Eli opened his mouth as if to argue, but then snapped it shut. He gave her a curt nod, and Abilene turned from him and all-but-fled to the ladies' restroom.

As the swinging door thumped behind her, she caught her reflection in the mirror. Her eyes were wide. Panicked. And pain still laced up and down her spine where Eli's hand had rested just seconds ago.

She was in trouble.

She had a feeling that the unpleasant sensations would continue to gain in intensity until . . . *what exactly?* She frowned into the mirror, deep lines appearing in her brow.

Unfortunately, the only time the pain got better was when Eli was touching her, and wasn't that just wonderful. If things got much worse, she might even resort to begging him for his touch, and after her little freak-out session yesterday morning in the abandoned house, she doubted he'd be excited by the idea.

"He's my *patient*. He's my *patient*," she chanted at her reflection. She splashed cool water on her face before heading back out into the Oklahoma sunshine.

Eli was leaning against the passenger side door of the truck with his arms crossed over his chest. It caused his t-shirt to pull across his pecs and biceps, and her mouth watered.

Damn, damn, damn!

"I'll drive for a while," he said gently. His tone was one he would use with a cornered animal, and Abilene knew that her behavior today was making her appear weak. Vulnerable. She *hated* that.

Eli opened the door for her with a pointed look, and Abilene made her way toward him, her feet dragging in the dirt parking lot. She couldn't stop herself from brushing against him as she got into her car. As her shoulder grazed across his chest, she shivered from the relief the action brought, then gritted her teeth as the pain came again while she settled into the seat.

Eli, of course, noticed. He swore in a low voice, but shut the door and made his way to the driver's seat. He sat still for a few seconds, his hands gripping the steering wheel.

"I, um, got something for you," he said. He sounded embarrassed and shy, a tantalizing combination Abilene realized regretfully seemed to be another thing that she couldn't resist in a man.

Eli dug his hand into his left hip pocket. It emerged a second later, and he extended it toward her. His fingers were clenched over something, and he turned his palm up and revealed what he held. Cradled in the palm of his hand was the turquoise bracelet Abilene had been staring at when Eli startled her earlier.

Abilene gasped. She reached out to brush her fingers over the stone, but Eli evaded her, turning his hand over to dangle the bracelet from his fingers. The move allowed her to take possession of the gift without having to touch him.

She didn't know if she was relieved or embarrassed to know he'd noticed her pain was touch-related. Maybe a bit of both. She gave him a wobbly smile as she slid the bracelet onto her wrist.

"It comes with a condition," Eli continued. She looked at him again. "Take these?" He now held a travel-sized portion of painkillers in one hand and, of all things, a Yoo-hoo in the other. Abilene felt herself fight tears as his thoughtfulness overwhelmed her. She freaking *loved* Yoo-hoo. "I know it's a kid's drink, but it always makes me feel better," he explained.

And Abilene felt herself fall a little bit for Eli.

"Shit," she whispered. He heard her.

"Um, I can get you something else to take the pills with, if you want," he said.

She snatched the bottle from him. "This is fine," she snapped. *Undone by a bottle of Yoo-hoo. Oh, how the mighty have fallen.*

Pain hit Abilene hard as her fingers brushed his, and she began to moan. She wrapped her arms around herself and doubled over as though she'd been punched in the gut.

***

Eli cursed frantically, his hands hovering over her shuddering form, even as he felt faint echoes of pain himself. He felt so helpless. He couldn't make this better. Touching would only make it worse.

You'll only make it worse if you stop *touching her once you've started.*

"Okay," he said in as calming a voice as he could manage, ignoring the Voice for now.

"Okay, Abilene, I'll get you to a bed as soon as I can. I promise," he said as he started the truck and peeled out.

"I want to sleep," she protested. "I just need to sleep. Please don't make me move again."

Hell, that was easy. He would drive until they ran out of road if that was all she wanted. "Shhh," he soothed. "You can do that. I won't stop for the night unless you give me the go-ahead, okay?"

She exhaled and curled into the window. Her breath fogged the glass in short bursts. Eli kept one anxious eye on her and one on the road until he noticed that her breaths had evened. She was already asleep.

Or had passed out. His muscles tightened even more. This was not okay. Abilene in pain was *not okay.*

He knew he'd promised her that he wouldn't touch her, but these were extenuating circumstances. Eli knew, just *knew*, the only reason he wasn't in as much pain as Abilene was because he had orgasmed this morning.

He couldn't just watch her suffer. He knew how to make it stop; he had to act. He kept anxious vigil over her as he pondered his next steps.

She began to stir about three hours later, and Eli held his breath as he waited to see what condition she was in after sleeping like the dead for the last couple hundred miles.

When she didn't begin moaning again, Eli took heart. Perhaps the pain had stopped.

"How are you feeling, baby?" he asked in a soft whisper, for some reason thinking his volume could prevent her further suffering.

Her head rolled on her shoulders until she was looking at him. Her hurt flashed in her eyes, and Eli's stomach dropped. *So, the pain's not gone, then.*

She offered him a weak smile. "It's not as bad as it was," she muttered, embarrassed to be discussing this with him. He was sure she'd prefer if he pretended he didn't know what was going on.

Yeah, well, that's not gonna happen, darlin'.

"Um," she licked dry lips, "is the offer of a bed still good?"

Eli was so relieved that she was offering him another way to help her that he took the first exit he could before even checking if they were in a town with a hotel. Fortunately, they had just pulled in to Ozark, Arkansas, and Eli saw the glowing sign for a Day's Inn as soon as he got to the bottom of the exit ramp.

"Almost there, darlin'," he told her as he pulled closer to the hotel. "Do you need anything to eat?"

She looked like she felt ill at the question. "Oh, God," she groaned, "no food."

"Shhh, okay, no food." He parked in the lot of the Day's Inn and tore out of the truck like a man possessed. He made it to the lobby in record time, and the desk clerk looked up warily as Eli barreled toward him.

Eli forced himself to calm down as he went about the business of securing a room for the night, but the clerk seemed to move as though he were stuck in a vat of molasses. As soon as Eli had the key in hand, he raced out of the lobby at a dead run. He knew he should be keeping a low profile, and his current behavior was anything but inconspicuous, but Abilene had given him something to do. He was damn well going to do it.

When he got back to the truck, Abilene was already leaning against the rear fender waiting for him. He'd missed getting to help her out of the car. *What help could you have been?* Maybe it was better for both of them that he hadn't been here to stand impotently by as she struggled against new onrushes of soreness.

"Alright, Abi, we're on the ground floor close to the lobby." He nodded in the direction from which he'd come, and Abilene began a painful shuffle to their door. Eli followed on her heels, pondering what he would do if she tripped. Fell. He hated it that he didn't have a ready answer. He resorted to a prayer-like repetition of *just make it to the door, make it to the door* in the absence of anything better to do.

When they arrived at their room, he fumbled with the key, his anxiousness causing his hands to shake, before throwing the door open, and allowing Abilene to continue into the room. She made her way to the closest bed and began to lower herself to the cheap duvet.

She lost her balance.

Everything went into slow motion. Abilene began to fall. She reflexively reached out to Eli just as he was doing the same toward her. Their hands grasped one another as Abilene crashed into the mattress, pulling Eli down with her. His weight crushed her as he fell onto her, their bodies pressed chest to thigh.

They both froze.

Oh, no, Eli's panicked mind raved at him. He should have been more careful. Should have stood further away. He was riddled with guilt, but the guilt was heaviest in the part of his mind that was rejoicing that he could feel every lush curve of her body pressed against him.

"Don't pull away," she moaned. "*Please.*" Tears filled her eyes. "It hurts so bad when you pull away." Her breath was shaky. One lone tear rolled down her cheek.

"God, baby, no," his voice was so rough, he wondered if he was fighting his own tears. She was wrecking him. "I won't pull away." *Ever.*

He was touching her. The effect on them both had been instantaneous. Abilene's brow had smoothed in the absence of her pain. The tiny aches Eli had been feeling condensed and rushed to his groin.

The damage was done. By a lucky mistake, he was touching her and wasn't allowed to stop. He knew he should just hold still; this was enough to keep the pain away. But no amount of reasoning could stop his hand from moving to her forehead to brush over her brow. His fingers traveled into her hair, and he wrapped one of her curls around his index finger.

She sighed in relief and turned into his palm. The feel of her beneath him was sweet torture. Her breasts felt exquisite. Her belly kept expanding and contracting with her breaths, and the feel of it surging and retreating against his own abdomen was driving him crazy. He wanted to feel it skin to skin.

Eli was harder than he'd ever been, and he was riding the razor's edge of control. He was cursing that promise he'd made her yesterday. He was able to stop her pain with just the simple touching they were currently doing. He couldn't in good conscience take this any further. As clichéd as it sounded, he respected her too much for that.

He never should have looked into her eyes. As soon as he did, she nibbled on her bottom lip, and that warm gaze dropped to his mouth.

Eli squeezed his eyes shut. Damn, he couldn't un-see that. *Just one kiss. You can stop at just one kiss.*

It was all the convincing Eli needed.

He lowered his head slowly, giving her plenty of time to turn away, but he saw her nostrils flare and her eyes flash. She wanted it, too.

He meant the kiss to be gentle, but as soon as he got his lips on hers, something inside of him snapped. His kiss became crushing. He would have worried that he was hurting her if she hadn't been returning his kiss just as fiercely. Her arms worked their way around him. One hand was threading fingers through his hair, and the fingernails of the other were digging into his back between his shoulder blades. The bite from that sensation spurred him on even more.

He angled his head, and Abilene knew where he was headed before he had to ask. She opened her lips for him, and he plunged into her warm mouth. She tasted better than ever; it was almost as if her passion had a flavor, and it was his new favorite. He groaned harshly at the taste, and thoughts of stripping off her jeans and panties and plunging into her bombarded him so violently that he tore his lips from hers, striving to put some space between them before he violated his promise to her. He immediately regretted the decision.

Abilene's eyes were dilated; only a thin ring of blue surrounded her pupils. Both Eli and Abilene were panting. He wanted so badly to just continue from where they'd stopped, but he knew better. He had no self-control where Abilene was concerned.

Abilene closed her eyes and began shaking. "Eli," she whispered brokenly, "I can feel it. The pain, it's coming back." Her eyes snapped back open.

What? "But we're touching," he objected dumbly. They were still pressed together; she should be fine. Right on cue, Eli felt the beginning echoes of his own pain, and damn, it was stronger than he'd ever felt it.

This was bad. Abilene's pain would be stronger than his if it followed the pattern it had all day. Eli bit back a grunt as what felt like a sucker punch landed in his lower back.

Abilene cried out. "Eli, it's worse!" Tears were trekking from the corners of her eyes into the blonde curls at her temples.

"Abi," he began. He had to stop when a fresh wave of pain traveled up his spine, stealing his breath. "I'm sorry, baby. This is my fault. I shouldn't have kissed you."

Her reply was a sob. "It h-hurts," she whimpered.

Damn it! The guilt was almost more intense than the pain. "Abilene," he hesitated. "I . . .know how to make the pain go away." He winced, both from the pain and from the words. Yup, they sounded as sleazy as he thought they would. "But . . . I made you a promise—" He didn't have the chance to finish his sentence before Abilene grabbed his shirt with both hands and jerked him toward her with surprising strength.

"*Please*," she begged, her eyes wide. "I don't care about that, just make it go away!" New pain wracked her, causing her back to bow. Her face twisted into a grimace, and her breaths became short and labored.

Promise be damned.

Eli shifted his weight until he was lying beside Abilene instead of on top of her. The movement caused her to panic. "Don't leave me!" she groaned.

Eli's gut twisted. "I'm not going anywhere, darlin'," he assured her. *As if I could walk away from this.* He'd wanted her so badly. Had his mind somehow known to stand too close to her, to kiss her, to pull away and guarantee that she would need him in the way he so desperately wanted to be needed?

"I'm a virgin," she moaned through gritted teeth.

He sucked in air. "What?" *Please let me have mis-heard that.*

"Just...seems like a ...good time to...tell you," she said as more tears leaked out of the corners of her eyes.

He groaned toward the ceiling. *A virgin?* Ah, God, why did he *love* that? But he couldn't take her virginity, especially like this.

She would never forgive him.

And that really mattered to him.

An idea popped into his head; there were other options—ways Eli could satisfy her and not . . . .

Eli moved one hand to the button of Abilene's jeans. He noticed that his hand was shaking, he was so damned nervous. He'd never had any complaints from his previous partners, but Eli realized with sudden clarity that they hadn't mattered. His hand was on *Abilene* now. His woman.

His woman who had never been with a man.

When Abilene undulated her hips under his hand, he realized that he'd been stalled out with his hand on her button for several moments. He had to get out of his head; Abilene was in pain, and he had been given the green light to fix it. No more hesitation.

With fumbling fingers, he unbuttoned her jeans and tugged her zipper down. His heart was pounding as sweet, cotton panties with a tiny bow at the top were revealed. His forced his eyes from the sight and looked at Abilene's face to gauge how she was doing.

One look at her face, and Eli knew she was out of her mind with anguish. Her eyes were squeezed shut; her mouth pinched and turned down at the corners.

Shit. He been so wrapped up in his own thoughts, contemplating every step like *he* was the freaking virgin, and in the meantime, Abilene's suffering had increased.

He quickly tugged her jeans down her hips. She helped him as much as she could by lifting her bottom from the bed, and soon, her jeans were around her knees. He noticed right away that her panties were soaked.

"Holy God," he whispered. This was the most glorious sight he'd seen in his entire life. He brought his hand up to the juncture of her thighs and brushed one finger over the wet fabric covering her core.

Abilene gasped in shock, and Eli, encouraged, moved his hand to cup her. She was so warm, her heat scorched him. He pressed the heel of his hand against the top of her cleft.

"Oh my God," Abilene whispered feverishly, her legs spreading as much as the jeans around her knees would allow. "More. Eli, *please* . . .more."

Oh yeah. Eli had no problem granting that request. He pondered sliding her panties down for half a second, but knew the moment he saw her bare, it would be over. Instead, he opted for working his hand under the elastic band at the top of her panties.

He closed his eyes as his fingers threaded through soft, soft curls. He held his breath as the tips of his fingers brushed moist flesh. And they both groaned in pleasure-pain as he parted that flesh and found her dripping with want.

"*Baby,*" he breathed. He moved closer to her and buried his face in her hair, trying to still the shaking that had started up again with a vengeance. "You're *killing* me. God, you're so wet."

She turned her head on the pillow until they were face-to-face once again. "Kiss me," she whispered, her breath fanning his face.

Yes, ma'am, he thought as he closed the gap between their lips. As soon as he was kissing her, she thrust her tongue into his mouth. She was taking charge, becoming demanding.

God, if she kept this up, he was lost. He maneuvered his hand deeper into her panties and began to work one finger toward her opening. She groaned into his mouth and thrust her tongue against his.

The pleasure was so intense he was worried that he was going to spill into his pants again, and before he'd taken care of her this time. *Not an option.* He pulled his aching erection away from its contact with her left hip to keep from thrusting, and it gave him just enough control to save himself.

Abilene rocked her hips forward and the tip of his middle finger dipped inside of her. He gritted his teeth, and Abilene moaned.

Eli worked his finger deeper inside of her. "So . . .tight . . ." he breathed against her lips. She was clamped so tightly around his finger that he could barely fit.

It was Abilene who got his finger all the way inside her. She rocked against his hand, moved against him, until his finger thrust past the clenched muscles.

She pulled her lips from his with a gasp to look up at him with awe in her eyes. "Holy shit," she whispered.

You can say that again. All of his worries about pleasing her faded into the background. She was so responsive, so in tune to what he was doing, he would have no problem making this good for her.

He smiled down at her, and she gave a shy smile back. He made sure to focus on her eyes before he began to withdraw his finger. Her breath hitched. When he had withdrawn almost completely, he thrust back into her all the way, grinding the heel of his hand against the swollen nub throbbing against his palm.

She cried out his name and arched her back. He did it again, and this time she rocked her hips into his thrust, bringing them both closer to the brink of release. He set a rhythm with his hand, and she matched it.

Abilene threaded the fingers of both hands into his hair and pulled him back down for a searing kiss. Their tongues moved in tandem with the thrusts, and Abilene's hips began to urge him to move faster.

Their breaths mingled. Eli could no longer keep from thrusting against her and moved close once again to grind against her hip.

God, everything felt so *good.* He'd never experienced anything like this before in his life, and he could see himself getting easily addicted to Abilene's body. To her responses. To the wet silk clenching and unclenching around his finger.

He circled her most sensitive spot with his thumb, and she came apart under his hand. He pulled from the kiss, not willing to miss a second of watching her come.

Her neck arched as her head kicked back for her to cry out with abandon. Her core clamped down on his finger, almost to the point of pain. Her nails dug into his biceps.

She was breathtakingly beautiful.

Eli worked furiously to memorize every detail. He wanted to remember this moment every day for the rest of his life.

When Abilene finally calmed, she looked at him askance, embarrassment blushing her cheeks.

Oh, no. He was going to put a stop to that emotion right now. He placed a soft kiss on her lips. "You were incredible," he whispered. "Abilene, I've never seen a more beautiful sight in all of my days."

Her blush deepened in color, but she smiled up at him. "*I* was incredible?" she asked with a teasing note in her voice. "I didn't know it could feel like that," she whispered, her smile fading as she noticed that he was still hard and aching against her hip. "You didn't. . . finish?" she asked hesitantly.

Eli raised one eyebrow. "Contrary to previous demonstrations, I don't always come in my pants like a teenager, darlin'," he murmured. Eli was trying to joke, to keep things light, but he could feel the pain lurking in the wings, waiting to overtake him again. He needed to slip away and take care of himself as soon as possible, but he couldn't bear to leave Abilene's side, yet.

"Do you want me to—" Abilene looked down, breaking eye contact. "I could . . . help you. Like you helped me." Her voice was so quiet that Eli thought maybe his mind had tricked him into thinking Abilene had just offered to take care of his problem for him. He stared at her for a few seconds, trying to remember if he'd seen her lips move.

"E-eli?" Abilene asked. "It was just an idea. I thought—" she broke off again and looked across the room.

Holy shit. She had. She'd actually said the words, and now he'd made her doubt herself because he was an idiot. He reached across her body and took her hand in his own. He tugged until he was able to press her hand against the front of his pants. His breath left him in an audible whoosh, and he allowed his desire for her to appear on his face uninhibited. Abilene swallowed, but her eyes met his once again.

"Baby, don't ever doubt how much I crave your hands on me. Anywhere. Under any circumstances." He pressed her hand more firmly against his length. "It's all I can seem to think about around you."

His words seemed to have their desired effect, and she moved her hand as though emboldened. Hell, this wasn't going to take long at all. He'd been on the brink moments ago as he watched her come. With one simple movement, she'd brought him right back to that edge.

She moved her hand out from under his, and for a moment he worried that she was going to change her mind. But instead, she pressed against his chest, pushing him onto his back beside her. She rose up on one elbow to look down at his body, and her eyes grew heated. "Can I . . .I want to see you, Eli." She was still blushing, but her hand moved to the hem of his t-shirt, making the meaning of her words clear.

She wanted to undress him.

Eli tried to make his movements casual. He figured tearing his clothes off in a rush might be a little frightening, but he was so eager to give her anything she wanted, especially this. He grabbed the hem of his shirt and pulled it over his head. He dropped it off the edge of the bed, then brought his eyes back to her face to see her reaction.

Her gaze was riveted to his chest, her hand following the direction of her gaze to stroke the valley between his pecs. It was a light touch, but Eli's stomach muscles clenched, and he bit back a groan.

Abilene jerked her hand away. "Did I hurt you? Is the pain back?" she asked in an anxious voice.

"No!" Eli blurted, startling her further. He took her hand and placed it back on his chest. "It's the farthest from *hurt* it can possibly be, baby. Trust me." As soon as her hand landed once again, his muscles restarted their shaking, but this time it made her smile.

"*I* do this to you?" Her voice held wonder, and a bit of pride. He nodded once, holding his breath as she grew more adventurous, stroking her hand down to his abdomen. She traced the ridges of his six-pack, and the slow movements were torturous. She was making her own time and gaining in confidence, but a very persistent part of his anatomy craved her attention.

As though she heard his thoughts, her eyes drifted to the bulge behind his fly. Her hand stilled over his belly button, and she began to nibble her lower lip. He could see excitement and nervousness mixed in her eyes.

"Do you want to see me there, too?" Eli asked. His voice was so low it was almost unrecognizable.

She nodded once. Eli moved his own hand to the button of his jeans, and Abilene's eyes flashed. He knew she was a doctor—hell, she'd even seen him naked before—but she looked terrified when Eli undid the button. He stopped.

"Hey," he whispered, reaching out to touch her cheek. "We can stop right here. Just say the word."

She shook her head. "No, I want to, just—" she closed her eyes and finished her sentence in a rush of words, "I-don't-know-what-I'm-doing-and-I-might-be-bad-at-it." She exhaled, relieved that she'd gotten it out.

Had he heard her right? Somehow he knew *Are you fucking kidding me?* was the wrong thing to say here.

"Oh . . . darlin' . . . you've got me on a hair trigger." He turned her face until she was forced to look at him. "I've almost come a million times since falling on top of you. Just touching you, the smell of your skin, the look on your face—" He brushed his thumb across her lower lip. "I can't *wait* to feel your hand on me. You couldn't be bad at it if you tried."

She gave him a brilliant smile and leaned down to kiss him. For once, he'd said the right thing. *Thank you, God.* As she deepened the kiss, her hand began a slow slide down to his fly. He felt a tugging, and the sound of the zipper ricocheted through the room.

And then, sweet God, she was touching him. The tentative brush of her fingertips almost ended everything right away.

She pulled away from the kiss to whisper, "Your pants . . . I can't quite . . . Will you push them down a bit?"

He rushed to comply, lifting his ass and shoving his jeans down his thighs in record time. She smiled into his eyes before looking down to the erection she held in her palm.

She gasped. "Oh my God." Her grip tightened, and Eli moaned. Loudly. "You're . . . *beautiful*," she whispered.

***

Abilene had never seen anything so incredible in her life. She couldn't tear her eyes from Eli's mostly naked body—a body that was like something out of a myth. The ache between her thighs throbbed for what she held in her hand.

There was no way any other man looked this good.

His chest and abdomen were packed with muscle. A happy trail started just below his belly button and thickened as it approached his erection.

Her eyes focused there, and the world faded away. This part of his body was more than she'd ever hoped for in a man. In her studies and examinations, she'd never found that part of a man's body attractive. It was functional. And, frankly, a little weird-looking.

But Eli—he was just breath taking. He was all smooth, velvety skin over hard, unforgiving length. His size was a little daunting—she couldn't quite fit her fingers all the way around him—but he was gorgeous.

She gave another experimental squeeze, and he groaned in that sexy guttural way he had when she'd done it the first time. When she slid her hand from the base to the plum-colored head, his hips kicked forward to follow her.

God, this made her feel powerful. Sexy.

She repeated the movement again, and this time, a single tear wept from the tip of his length. His groan was more desperate this time, but Abilene didn't notice. All she could see was that glistening droplet.

Her mouth watered to taste it. To taste him.

Would he let her? She looked at his face and was struck by the expression he wore. His eyes were hooded and glazed. His lips were parted and wet, as though he'd been licking them while she had been focusing her attention elsewhere. His breaths were coming in pants

In a second, she knew he would let her do anything to him she wanted. And she wanted her mouth on him.

She began by kissing his chest while she gathered her courage. His breathing changed. When she moved down to his stomach, he brought a hand up to the back of her head.

"Abi . . .baby, what're you—"

She was about to lose her nerve, so she went for it. She closed her eyes and pressed a tentative, open-mouthed kiss where the droplet of moisture lay.

"*Fuck*," Eli moaned harshly, his back arching off the bed, and his fingers tangling in her hair.

Abilene groaned from deep in her chest. God, he tasted . . . *amazing*. She licked her lips, then licked him with the flat of her tongue from base to tip, relishing every new flavor.

"I can't . . .believe you're—" Eli was panting desperately. "Abilene . . .it's so . . .*God!*"

He reached down and grabbed her jeans, tearing them the rest of the way off her legs. "I'm not coming without giving you this, too." He grabbed her by the thighs and swung her around until her knees where planted on each side of his head.

Abilene panicked and tried to squirm away. He placed both hands on her ass. "Abi, *please*," his hands squeezed as punctuation. "Let me taste you, too. I want to so badly." He leaned his head up and placed a kiss on her panties where they covered her aching core.

Sensation shot through her, stronger than anything she'd ever felt. She arched her back into his kiss, sighing with pleasure. Her embarrassment began to fade, and she didn't protest when Eli hooked one finger beneath the crotch of her panties to pull them aside.

"Oh, *shit*," he murmured, and Abilene stiffened. Was something wrong? Was he turned off by what he saw? She renewed her struggles, and Eli shushed her and prevented her from moving away.

He brushed a finger over the folds he had pleasured earlier— intimate skin he now could see plainly—and she froze. "Abilene," he began, "you're the most exquisite woman I've ever seen." He leaned in closer and blew a gentle stream of air over her moist flesh.

Abilene cried out. The pleasure was so intense that tears sprang to her eyes. She buried her face in his groin to steady herself. When he jumped beneath her, she remembered that she had a part to play in this, too.

It was the thought of putting her mouth on him once again that calmed her. She hadn't gotten enough of him, and she relished the idea of getting to kiss and lick him some more.

She wrapped her hand around his base and took the tip of him into her mouth to suck lightly. It had the same effect on Eli as slapping the hind end of a horse. He jerked into motion, pressing his mouth over her swollen clit, pushing Abilene right up to the edge of orgasm.

All embarrassment vanished. This just felt right. Perfect. Molten hot.

She took more of him into her mouth, and when he groaned this time, she felt it vibrate against her. She undulated her hips, and he squeezed his hands encouragingly and licked her. Things fell out of control. Abilene began to move her mouth at a frantic pace, the desperation she was feeling in the pit of her stomach manifesting itself in a frenzy of motion. Eli grunted and set his own brutal pace, his face pressing against her, his lips and tongue driving her to new heights. Talk was impossible, but her mind was screaming at her, telling her that she'd never felt anything like this, that Eli was changing everything, that she was falling for him, beginning to . . .*love* him.

Eli pulled his mouth away to groan, "Baby, you need to pull away—" He tried to move away from her mouth, but she tightened her grip and took him more deeply. His whole body jerked, and his voice grew desperate. "Abi, I'm going to . . . ." She curled her upper body around his erection and moaned against him to let him know she wanted *all* of him. He cried out and buried his face between her thighs once again to plunge his stiffened tongue inside her.

The moment she felt him jet hotly at the back of her throat, she lost it, too. She ground against his face, stars flashing behind her eyes, as she swallowed everything he had to give her.

When she collapsed against him, her breaths harsh and ragged, he reached down to gather her into his arms, rotating her until she was nestled against his side with her head tucked under his chin.

She could hear his heart pounding and knew that her own was beating out a similar rhythm. He was holding her so tightly, yet his grip was gentle, caring. He pressed a kiss into her curls and squeezed her even tighter.

"Abilene, this is going to sound crazy—" When she tried to sit up, he put a hand to her shoulder to prevent it. "We've only known each other for three days, but . . .I think I . . . . Something is making me . . . . I'm falling for you."

She felt him wince at the words—the admittedly crazy words— and she brushed his hand aside and sat up despite his protests.

"You can't mean that," she whispered. He certainly *looked* like he meant it. A part of her was overjoyed with his confession, another part was offended that he hadn't been able to say it without wincing, and the biggest part was overwhelmed with a sense of foreboding.

"I think it's time we had no more secrets between us," he said, his brow furrowing in resignation. And then he said the words that make every woman's heart stop.

"Abilene, I have something to tell you."

Chapter Eleven

Abilene watched in mute apprehension as Eli extricated himself from her arms, pulled his pants back up, and moved to the other bed. She immediately felt cold and missed his closeness, but she was more worried by his sudden change in mood.

He settled himself on the edge of the opposing bed, facing her, his elbows on his knees. He wouldn't meet her eyes.

"I need to tell you why I was in that medical facility," he said to the floor between his feet.

Abilene sat up and backed up to the headboard. She drew her knees to her chest and wrapped her arms around her legs to clasp her hands in front of her shins. She desperately wished her pants were within arm's reach; the intimacy of her lack of clothes felt out-of-place.

"Didn't you already tell me why you were there?" she asked, not quite wanting to dreg up the story she hadn't believed entirely in the first place.

Eli didn't respond right away.

"Eli," Abilene made her voice stern. "What didn't you tell me?" She had a sick feeling in her stomach.

He scrubbed a hand down the front of his face and straightened. "I told you I was a prisoner, but I didn't tell you why." He exhaled and looked her in the eye. "Abilene, I was a test subject for the fruit from the Tree of Everlasting Life."

She blinked at him. *The . . . Tree of Everlasting Life?* He sat for several seconds, letting her digest what he'd just said. "You mean, like from that *story* you made me tell the first night?" she asked, emphasizing the word *story* with a heavy dose of disbelief.

He sighed, her reaction obviously what he had expected. "Yes, Abilene, like from the *story*. Which, I might add, a good deal of the world's population believes was recorded from historical *fact*."

Yeah, the uneducated, religious part of the world's population. "Eli—" she began, but had to stop. The sick feeling in her stomach was growing. She suddenly didn't care if she had to walk to Alaska to get her pants, she couldn't stand to be undressed in front of him anymore. She scrambled from her spot at the headboard to snatch her pants from the floor between the beds. She pulled them on in jerky movements, then resumed her defensive pose against the headboard once again. Eli watched the proceedings with resignation in his eyes.

When the heavy silence between them grew too uncomfortable to bear, Abilene tried speaking again. "I don't know what you want me to say." She couldn't look at him.

"Are you willing to listen to the whole story?" he asked.

She wasn't, but she felt her head nodding anyway.

"Okay, I'll start at the beginning," he said, almost to himself. But then he remained quiet. Finally, she forced her eyes to his face. His expression was imploring, but defiant. "Just, try to keep an open mind," he admonished.

She nodded again.

"You know we've been at war in the Middle East for decades. Well, right after 9/11, rumors began to circulate that some American soldiers had stumbled upon what they swore were the remains of the Garden of Eden."

He laughed without humor. "Everyone thought they were crazy. It became this huge joke among those of us stationed in Afghanistan. I mean, come on, the Garden of Eden in the middle of the fucking desert?" He shook his head, then shrugged. "But the rumors reached the right ears in Washington. A year later, a small troop of us were ordered to excavate the site those soldiers marked for us on a map."

He seemed to get caught up in the story. "We didn't mind. By that time, the fervor of the American public after 9/11 had died down. We weren't heroes anymore, just invaders. We jumped at the chance to break from our boring, everyday duties."

His eyes flashed and he clenched his fists. "But the moment we pulled up to the site, every single one of us knew—" He swallowed. "Abilene, it just *felt* different.

"There were only five of us, and we just sat in that Humvee, staring at each other, no one willing to say what each of us was thinking: that the rumors might have been true. That we were about to step foot in the *Garden of Eden*.

"I don't remember who got out first, but we all just sort of *followed* this pull. It was almost like the trees were tugging us toward them."

Trees? Abilene's mind latched on to that word. Plural. As in, more than one.

Eli continued, "We could definitely tell we were in the remnants of a garden, the biggest garden any of us could ever imagine. We could make out the skeletons of different plots—flowers, vines, vegetables. It looked like a burned out, scorched—" Eli paused to search for a word. "*Graveyard.*"

He took a deep breath. "And then we came to the center of the garden. Instead of sand, we were standing on dry, cracked mud. It crumbled under our boots. And poking up through the cracks like they had been buried?" His voice got very quiet. "The tips of tree branches."

Eli stopped talking for a few moments. He seemed lost in memory. He shook his head twice, took a shuddering breath, and continued in a tired voice. "We reported back what we had found, and I don't know why we didn't expect it, but they came for us in the middle of the night. Just," he made a grabbing motion with his hands, "snatched us from our bunks and tossed us in the back of a truck.

"We were stateside by the next evening, meeting with a damned general. We were told our lives were over. Officially speaking. They offered us an ultimatum: they could make us disappear—and we all knew what that meant—or we could sign on to become a part of Operation: Middle of the Garden and they would compensate our loved ones. We were told that no matter what we chose, our families would be notified that we had been killed in action.

"Every single one of us signed up to join. My mom had just been diagnosed with cancer, and the compensation they promised ensured I was more help to her dead. Only one other soldier, Jericho and I were brought to a hospital. We never saw the other three soldiers again."

Abilene cinched her legs in tighter. She wanted to comfort him. She wanted to run from him screaming. She wanted to believe him. She couldn't.

"They called the fruit a *specimen*," Eli continued. "Just slipped it in with all of the pills and supplements they made us take. We never knew what had happened—until the change hit. The next morning, we woke up and couldn't even recognize ourselves.

"I mean, we were in pretty good shape to start with. I was a new Green Beret, and Jericho was athletic. But something had happened to us." He motioned to his body, and flashes of his perfect physique appeared in front of Abilene's eyes. She stared at his flawless chest.

"As soon as the scientists saw us, they separated us. We were put in two different labs. And then the . . .*experiments* . . .began.

"The first one was easy," he said. Abilene knew this was hard for him. Maybe even as hard for him to tell it as it was for her to hear it and feel the hope leak out of her.

"It was lethal injection," Eli said. Abilene's eyes snapped to his face. Oh, God, what had he been through that these were his memories?

"I just . . .fell asleep. I barely remember it. I woke two days later and had lost all memory. It wasn't until they were preparing to do the second experiment that I remembered they had killed me. That they were planning to kill me again . . . .

"Abilene, that's what the experiments were." Eli's voice was rough, achy. "No matter what they did to me, no matter how I died," his voice cracked, "I always came back. They gave me the fruit from the Tree of Life, and it made me immortal."

Oh-God-oh-God-oh-God. Abilene squeezed her eyes shut and resisted the urge to rock back and forth in sorrow. She felt tears sting her eyelids. This was worse than anything she could have imagined. *He's broken. The man you thought you were falling for is insane.*

It was such a cruel end to such a hopeful day.

Abilene straightened her spine. She would *not* show her despair in front of him. He had started off as her patient, and he certainly needed medical attention now. She had an oath to fulfill. This delusion about death and immortality could be the symptom of several things: post traumatic stress disorder, definitely—even schizophrenia, a zealous upbringing, or child abuse.

She knew one of the rules in psychology was not to deny what the patient believed. *Okay, so what should I do?* She opted for a question.

"Eli, how many times have you . . .died?" She hadn't been able to say the word without hesitating first, and Eli noticed.

He chose not to comment on her hesitation and answered the question. "Latest count is 140 times. You found me right after the last experiment."

That gave her pause. She remembered those moments in the closet vividly. They had marked the transition in her life, a time she would recall divided her life into *Before* and *After*.

She had declared him dead.

No, she'd already decided she must have been mistaken. She'd told herself so several times since he had awoken from his . . .*coma*.

"Do you a-age?" Abilene asked.

Eli shook his head once.

"So, you've been alive for...." She waited for him to fill in the blank.

"Thirty-eight years."

He expected her to believe that he was nearly forty? Wasn't it just yesterday that she was thinking he looked her age or younger?

"Okay," she said, "are there any other side effects from the specimen?" *Phew.* She'd made it through that question without a single hesitation.

His shoulders drooped, but he just sat there, staring at the floor.

"Eli?" she prodded.

He shook his head.

•••

Abilene looked devastated.

Hell, you happy now? Eli asked the Voice.

Yes, it answered back smugly.

"I understand," said Abilene with finality. Uh oh, that wasn't good. "Eli, I'm going to help you. We'll go to Atlanta tomorrow, back to your hometown where everything is familiar, and we'll find a great place for you."

Eli's patience broke. "'A place for me,'" he repeated. "You mean another hospital where I'll be a prisoner." He surged to his feet. "Damn it, Abilene, I tell you I think I might love you or something, then tell you the *truth* about myself, and you want to have me committed!"

She'd been so wary about him just seconds ago that he half expected her to cower in the wake of his anger. Instead, in the true Abilene-form he'd come to admire so much, she stood, too, toe-to-toe with him.

"'Or something'?" she yelled into his face. "Jeez, Eli, if your feelings for me are so distasteful, why don't you try to fight them?"

"Don't you think I have?" he yelled right back. "*God*, I want to *hate* you, woman! You're everything I despise!"

She reeled back as though he'd slapped her.

Shit! Shit, shit, shit!

Really, Eli? the Voice drawled. *You're a regular silver-tongued Casanova.*

He opened his mouth to apologize, not knowing what he could say to make it better, but Abilene held up a hand to stop him.

"No, it doesn't matter," she said hoarsely. "*I* should apologize. That was very unprofessional of me."

Eli did not like her tone at all. It was distant. Cold.

"I can promise you that we will have a perfectly acceptable doctor/patient relationship from now on, Eli. You can trust me."

She actually sounded like she had something to apologize for. As though their relationship up to this point had been a mistake. An unethical move on her part.

It hurt more than Eli expected it would.

She wasn't done yet. "It's been a long day. I think it's time we went to bed." She sat down stiffly on the bed he'd pleasured her on just half an hour ago. She gave him a look that told him not to contemplate joining her there.

He sat down obediently on the other bed, dumbfounded by how wrong things had gone. He'd damaged them. Damaged what they'd begun to cultivate.

"I'll see you in the morning. Good night," she said in clipped tones. She reached to the bedside table and clicked off the light.

As his eyes adjusted to the dark, he watched her lie back and roll onto her side, presenting him with her back.

He should lie down, too. Should try to get some sleep. He would need it if he were going to protect her.

But he couldn't look away from her rigid back.

And so he didn't miss it when her back began to shake with silent sobs.

He felt sick. He could do nothing but watch as she cried until she fell into an exhausted sleep.

Even then, he couldn't break his paralysis to allow his own worn body to fall back to the bed and into slumber.

He was frozen in place, haunted by what had just happened, until the rising sun began to stream in through the window.

Chapter Twelve

This was quickly turning out to be one of the worst mornings of Eli's life. Abilene had said not one blessed word to him since waking up on the textbook definition of "the wrong side of the bed." At least it was a textbook definition in Eli's mind since the side she'd woken up on was not next to him.

She hadn't attacked him, verbally or physically. Hadn't indicated in any way whatsoever that she was angry with him. No, that would have been a relief.

Instead, she'd treated him with the cold, calculated distance of a doctor with her crazy and wayward patient. She'd nodded politely when he suggested it was time to hit the road; she'd smiled each time he'd tried to engage her in small talk in the last couple of hours.

She was driving him fucking nuts.

But he'd be damned if he was going to attempt conversation again. He wasn't quite ready to admit how much it hurt to have her write him off. He didn't need a constant reminder that he'd botched his declaration last night.

Anything, literally *anything* would have been better than the actual way he'd chosen to let Abilene know about his feelings.

Well, it was bound to happen sooner or later. He'd been doing well in the wooing department, considering he and Abilene had met when he decided to kidnap her. He just wasn't that smooth. That he had managed to charm her was a miracle in-and-of itself.

And now, the glacial chill emanating from her corner of the truck was causing him to lose hope. Eli had no idea how to get back in the good graces of a woman; he'd never tried before. In his previous life, if he'd driven a woman away, he'd never bothered to win her back. There was no point, and there hadn't been a woman so special that he had even considered it.

Not so with Abilene. From the second her face fell because of his words, Eli craved reconciliation. Well, not so much reconciliation as the ability to turn back time and kick his own ass before he screwed up.

Abilene straightened in her seat, and for a moment, Eli felt his heart rate quicken at the thought that she was getting ready to break her reign of silence.

She gestured to a car parked on the shoulder about half a mile ahead of them. "Maybe we should stop and see if they need help," she said. "We're out in the middle of nowhere."

He squinted through the windshield. *Hmmm.* He didn't like the thought of stopping to help someone when Abilene was in the car. If he was by himself, sure, but if the stranded driver proved to be less-than-savory, he didn't want Abilene anywhere near potential danger.

However it *was* the first time she'd spoken to him all day, and he didn't have any better ideas on how to begin mending fences. And she was right. They were in the middle of nowhere. It could be hours before another car passed by.

He grunted to let her know he'd heard her as he began to slow down in preparation for pulling off to the side. He was overthinking this; it would be nothing. They would help some sweet old lady change a tire and then be on their way, and Eli would look like a hero.

As the tires of the truck kicked up the gravel from the shoulder, Eli spied the parted hair of a fastidiously groomed man and relaxed. It was just an older gentleman. The other driver's window was rolled down, and he was studying them in his rearview mirror.

Eli turned to Abilene. What he was about to ask was not going to win him any favors. "If I ask you really nicely, will you stay in the truck?"

She looked offended at his request—it was obvious that a man asking the lil' lady to stay put was not her favorite—but she nodded, anyway.

Eli took a deep breath, opened the door, and stepped outside into the Arkansas morning.

"Uh, hey there," he called. "Do you need help?"

The man sitting in the car turned his head at the sound of Eli's voice, and at the sight of the shadowy profile, Eli froze.

Tormentor.

He knew, in the flash of a heartbeat, the man in the car was Major Taylor.

Oh, holy God, what have I done? Abilene was sitting in the truck behind him. He'd hand-delivered the most precious person in the world to the most hateful.

With fluid movements, Major Taylor swept open the door of his car and unfolded to his full height. Eli sunk back on his heels, adopting a fighting stance.

"Well, well, well," Major Taylor said. "I must say, I didn't expect getting you to pull over to be so easy an endeavor." He stepped forward. "I was hatching hair-brained plots of chasing you down and forcing you from the road."

"I will rip you limb from limb, even if she has to watch," Eli growled from the back of his throat. He didn't want Abilene to witness him exacting his revenge, but if the Tormentor took one more step toward him, and therefore her, he was going to seal his own fate.

Major Taylor sighed. "You always were so primitive, Subject." He shook his head in mock-sorrow while reaching into the inside pocket of his blazer.

Flashes of red rage lit behind Eli's eyes as he realized that Major Taylor was pulling out a small, deadly firearm.

And then, from behind him, Eli heard the sound of Abilene exiting the truck. Horror washed through him.

"Eli?" she asked in a wavering voice. The timbre of her voice portrayed an array of worry, and it struck him like a blow that she was concerned for his safety. *His* safety; not her own "Ah, right on time, my dear," Major Taylor said, turning his attention toward where she stood.

Eli stepped between Major Taylor and his line-of-sight to Abilene. "You don't get to talk to her," he said.

He nearly jumped out of his skin when he felt Abilene's light touch on his shoulder. She had scooted around the hood of the truck and now stood at his back in a sign of solidarity.

It meant more to him than she could have guessed.

"Well, if the pleasantries are to be denied us, I may as well get to the point," the Tormentor said. "Abilene is coming with me."

"That's not a possibility."

"I was certain that would be your response." Major Taylor's voice returned to its light tone, but his face remained resolute. "Abilene, dear, I apologize ahead of time for what I'm about to do." With no further indication that he was about to act, Major Taylor raised his gun, leveling it at Abilene.

The only thought Eli was capable of was *he's pointing a gun at Abilene.* He barreled toward Major Taylor in that same second.

The sound of the gun firing reverberated through Eli's chest and bounced across the asphalt of the freeway.

Eli didn't even slow down.

He missed. He actually missed.

Disbelief in his luck strengthened his speed. In the next moment, Eli had his hand wrapped around the Tormentor's wrist. With a simple movement, Eli forced the Tormentor's arm to bend mid-forearm, the resulting snap of bone accompanied by a masculine scream.

"You don't *ever,*" Eli glared into the pain-glazed eyes of Major Taylor, "point a gun at my woman."

Eli punctuated his words with a merciless twist of the arm still clutched in his hand. Major Taylor moaned in abject pain and fell to his knees at Eli's feet.

The headiness of having the Tormentor at his mercy filled Eli's head with orgasmic-like pleasure. Eli's eyes roved Taylor's writhing form, looking for the next point of attack. The next place to inflict pain.

"*Eli!*"

He froze. His brain was so taken with his current task that he couldn't place the anguished cry, but it stopped him in his tracks, the primal part of him responding to the pain he heard. The pain that was not coming from the pathetic man at his feet.

He turned, his feet sluggish.

What he saw took years off his immortal life.

Abilene stood on swaying feet where he'd left her. Her eyes were shocked wide open. Her nostrils flared in panic. Her fists were clenched together in a white knuckled grip below her breasts.

She was covered in blood.

The source of the blood seemed to be centralized beneath her fisted hands, but it splattered across her chest and dribbled down her abdomen to her thighs. Specs of red dotted her cheeks, clung to her eyelashes, wet her hair.

"Eli," her lips ghosted without air.

"*No.*" Eli was at her side in a moment.

He heard the sounds of Major Taylor scrambling to his car on his knees, the cranking of an engine, and the fading sound of a car fleeing the scene, but he paid it no mind. His world was focused on the current realization of his worst nightmare.

"No," he repeated, giving her a slight shake. "Where are you hit?" He didn't wait for her to answer, but pulled her hands from the large spread of blood covering her front.

He stepped back in confusion.

He had expected to find a singed entry hole marring the front of Abilene's shirt. He felt disconnected from his body as he brushed shaking fingers over blood-soaked, but otherwise unmarred, material.

He brought his eyes to her face once again.

"Where are you hit?" he repeated, enunciating each word.

Her lips moved without sound a few times before she was able to stutter, "Y-you."

Dizziness was preventing Eli from understanding what she was saying. Eli shook his head in an attempt to clear the cobwebs.

"It's you," Abilene clarified, her voice infused now with strength. "You're the one who's hit."

Eli's hands fell from Abilene's arms, their weight far too much for his muscles to handle.

He followed her riveted stare down to his own chest and noticed that a clean entry wound lay between his own pecks; an almost dainty trickle of blood trailed down to the hem of his shirt.

"Oh."

The pain rushed in as though it had been waiting for Eli to acknowledge its source before attacking. Eli grunted; his knees locked, and he swayed forward. Abilene tried to catch him, but even more surprisingly, she managed it. Her petite hands grasped him at his shoulders, and he scrambled to relocate his center of gravity so he wouldn't fall and crush her.

His brain scrambled to make sense of what had happened, of the blood covering Abilene from head to toe.

She had been standing right behind him when he had bolted toward Taylor. The blood covering her must be from his exit wound. God, if she looked like this . . .his back must be . . . *gone.*

It was a fatal wound. Ask him how he knew.

Okay, time was of the essence here. The last time he'd taken a gunshot wound to the chest, he'd expired within minutes. A similar wound made by the same gun would guarantee similar results.

Major Taylor could grow a pair and come back at any moment. Abilene would soon be unprotected. Eli had to do everything in his power to ensure that she would be safe when he was gone.

"Truck," he rasped through dry lips. "Please," he added as an afterthought once he saw the dinner-plate size of her eyes.

Abilene's head nodded twice, and she maneuvered herself under his left armpit. She then stalled out, not sure of where to put her arm since his back was a mess.

Eli took over for her. He leaned as much weight as he dared on her shoulders and began to move forward, shuffling to the truck. There was no way he would make it around the hood to the passenger's side, so he just headed to the driver's side.

His forward motion seemed to jar Abilene from her shock; she hooked a thumb through the middle belt loop of his jeans and did her best to keep him from crumpling to the ground.

He half expected to die before reaching the truck: his vision was tunneling, and the telltale coldness of death was emanating from the central location of his heart. But they made it, and Abilene somehow got him into the truck, followed him inside, and got him to lay flat across the seat with his head in her lap.

Somewhere in the dim recesses of his fading consciousness, he recognized that she was touching him again. Apparently, all it took to get her forgiveness was a horrific death. He'd have to remember that for the future.

"Drive . . .into the trees," he directed in a fading voice.

"Eli, we have to get you to the hospital!" she countered. "This is bad. I won't be able to stop the bleeding. You need surgery—". He forced his eyes to focus on her face and saw the devastation that covered her features. Tears flooded her eyes, but she refused to let them spill.

He was confused. *Why is she upset?* For Eli, death was not the end. She knew that.

He shook his head at her. "Drive, please. Get off . . .road."

She seemed to remember that moments ago, they were face-to-face with a willing-to-commit-murder psychopath. "Okay, that's a good idea." She cranked the truck, and he could tell from the sounds of the tires that she was moving the truck off-road to the continuous line of trees that lined the Arkansas freeway.

He closed his eyes for a moment and woke several moments later to painful shaking.

"Eli!" Abilene was screeching in his ear. He pried his eyes open to find that he was out of the truck. He was flat on his back beneath the canopy of trees. "Don't you *dare* close your eyes again," she commanded in a panic.

He couldn't promise her that. He'd gotten her as safe as was possible, given the circumstances, and the familiar pull of death was lurking in the wings. He'd done the best he could, and it wasn't nearly good enough.

He tried to raise his hand to touch her, but it fell to his side. Abilene read his intent, picked up his hand, and cradled it against her cheek. With devastation, he realized he couldn't feel the smooth skin beneath his palm. It would have been so great to just *feel* her once more.

"I-I'm sorry," he whispered. *For so much.* He was sorry for kidnapping her, for exposing her to danger, for getting himself killed and leaving her vulnerable. But most of all, he was sorry for not telling her how he felt about her in the way she deserved.

He closed his eyes once more, the heavy weight tugging on his body too much to ignore any longer.

"Eli, no," Abilene pleaded. "*Please*, fight it."

Eli reveled in the feeling of having her near. This death was different—not as hopeless—because she was here. He wasn't alone.

He wished he had the energy to say he was sorry one more time, but it was over. He heard Abilene begin to sob and wondered once more why she was so distraught. He'd told her—

But she didn't believe you.

Death pulled him under.

***

Major Taylor cradled his destroyed arm against his chest and used his knees to steer. He was swerving all over the road, but in the back roads of Arkansas, no one would see him. He was off the map.

He kept reliving the firing of the gun. How had he missed at point-blank range?

He had failed to secure the female. And now he had to contact his associate and admit that he was coming in alone. And injured.

He moved his knees to steer the car to the shoulder. When he had to remove the brace of his good arm to retrieve his cell phone, his mangled arm flopped with a *thwap* against the steering wheel.

Major Taylor cried out in the cab of the car. The horror of watching his arm flap around from a joint that had not existed an hour ago was almost enough to have him blacking out. It was only the gravity of having to report that kept him lucid.

He groaned as he lifted his hips just enough to reach the cell phone in his back pocket, and gritted his teeth from more than the pain as he listened to the dial tone hum in his ear.

His assistant answered after one ring. "That was quick. When can I expect you?"

The phone call was already as hard as Major Taylor had anticipated it would be. He fought to keep the fear and pain from his voice as he said, "There's been a complication."

He could hear the hesitation crackling over the line. "A complication," his assistant said as though trying to find meaning to words that were in a different language.

Major Taylor sighed. "I don't have them." His head fell back against the seat rest.

More silence. Finally, "You don't have them."

The throbbing agony radiating out from his arm mixed with his frustration and had his head snapping back up. "Repeating everything I say does us no good!" he snapped, craning the phone around so his lips brushed the receiver as he spoke.

"Well, honestly, sir, it isn't as though we could be doing any worse."

Major Taylor growled into the phone. "You *will* watch your tone. I am your superior officer."

He must have put a significant amount of threat behind his tone, because his assistant responded with an immediate, "Yes, sir."

It was not without a wave of relief that Major Taylor allowed himself a steadying breath. He didn't deserve the deference of his assistant, but by some stroke of luck he'd gotten it.

"You can continue to expect me around the same time," Major Taylor continued after a moment. "And I will still need the operating room." Shame made his pause before revealing his current predicament. "I require surgery for an injury," he said as quietly as possible.

"I'm sorry," his assistant said. "What was that?"

Major Taylor gathered strength beneath his diaphragm, hoping to infuse his voice with power. "My arm is—" he glanced at the green and blue bruising already mottling his forearm. "I'm injured," he finished simply. Best to save the extent of his injury until he could see his assistant face-to-face.

If he was expecting his condition to garner sympathy, he was bound for disappointment. "Yes, sir," his assistant said, sarcasm and a tone of disrespect weaving back into the voice ringing in Major Taylor's ear.

Major Taylor didn't dare tempt fate a second time by reminding his assistant to respect him; he ended the phone call.

As he stared through the windshield with bleary eyes at the road leading to Georgia, his body begged him for sleep. For a reprieve.

But there was no time. He needed medical attention, but perhaps more importantly, he needed a plan. This situation may be beyond salvageable, but that didn't mean that Major Taylor wasn't going to give it a try.

Chapter Thirteen

She couldn't stop running her fingers through his hair. Eli's skin had long ago lost the warmth and vitality of life, and yet she couldn't quit touching him.

Abilene had fought with the meager tools she had to revive Eli. But there was only so much CPR could do, and reconstructing massive wounds and restoring blood loss were not on the list.

How was it possible that she was hunched over Eli's body for the second time in three days?

This time, though, he really was dead.

She'd had an up-close-and-personal look at what that bullet had done to Eli's body. The evidence was still splattered on her clothes.

And she couldn't ignore the irrefutable proof of watching him take his last breath. That image was still emblazoned on her corneas. She feared she would never see anything else.

But the feel of his hair running through her fingers was still the same, and so she would stay here, looking into his face—the only part of him that didn't portray a horrific death—for as long as she wanted.

She suspected that would be forever.

She hadn't cried yet. The sorrow was too severe for tears. What she had done was re-examine her every cruel action since Eli's bombshell revelation of the night before.

So he'd botched it. Badly. He hadn't said anything she herself hadn't been feeling. Falling for someone after three days? Asinine. She knew that, and he was smart enough to know it, too.

But. He'd had the courage to tell her what he felt—doubts and all. She'd only had the courage to realize that she cared for him the moment his eyes had glazed over in death.

When he'd died, she'd managed to tear his shirt down the middle, using the rip from the bullet hole as a starting point, to examine his chest for any telltale sign of respiration.

There had been none.

Since then, she had ignored the freakishly neat hole marring the perfection of Eli's body. Now she couldn't prevent a quick flick of her eyes. She braced herself for the physical blow of seeing his wound again. As soon as her eyes touched the wound, she moved them to his face again.

She frowned. Her fingers froze in his hair.

Her eyes raked down his face again, down the length of his neck, over his collarbone, to rest on his chest.

Where's the wound?

She stared for several long seconds at the smooth skin covering packed muscle. A small splatter of blood and the trickle that ran down his abdomen were still present, but the actual bullet hole was . . . *gone.*

She sucked in a breath and blinked, trying to clear her vision of what had to be an optical illusion.

She looked again, only to find that she was right. Abilene couldn't find the wound because, well, there *wasn't* a wound.

She snatched her hand from Eli's hair and scrambled back a few feet until her back bumped against the trunk of a tree.

Oh, God. I'm going crazy! It had finally happened. The stress of the past few days had taken its toll. It had been inevitable. But this—to have her mind play tricks on her in this way—it was cruel.

She wanted him to be alive, and her throttled brain was doing its best to give that wish to her.

Help him.

She looked to the canopy of trees. Peered through the checkered shade of the forest. It took her a few moments to realize that no one was here; no one had spoken to her.

She squinched her eyes shut. The Voice that had first whispered, *The One,* to her. It was back.

Help him, it repeated, more forcefully this time.

"He's *dead,*" she retorted aloud, wincing at the sound of her voice and its note of desperation.

Yes, it said simply. *Help him.*

With small, painful movements, Abilene crawled back to Eli's side. Help him, the Voice had said. But how?

She brushed her fingers over his sternum, expecting to feel some indication that he had recently suffered a fatal wound. Her fingers found perfectly knit bone and skin. There was not even an indentation in the clean circle centering the blood splatter.

And Eli's skin was warm.

Not quite normal temperature warm, but certainly warmer than it had been minutes ago.

Abilene's now-shaking hands moved to Eli's shoulder, and she struggled with his dead weight until she was able to get him to roll over. And then she gazed in amazement at his back.

The giant crater of carnage left behind from the bullet's devastating exit was shrinking before her eyes. Eli's skin, muscle, and bone were . . . *regenerating.* That was the only way she could think to describe it. Eli's wound was healing, but it was doing so as such a quick rate that Abilene could measure its progress visually. What would have taken months in a regular medical case would be finished in mere minutes.

"Holy shit," she breathed through parted lips. She looked at the profile of Eli's face, recalling the unbelievable story he had told her last night. "You weren't lying to me," she whispered to him. She closed her eyes and tilted her head back. "You're not crazy."

She didn't know whether she was referencing Eli or herself, but the relief that neither of them were candidates for intense psychological evaluation warmed her just like the rays of sunshine that shone down through the breaks in the leaves.

And then she realized what this meant.

Eli was coming back.

Her fingers clutched Eli's shoulder. She remembered the first time she'd seen him. She remembered the "recovery" her mind hadn't allowed her to accept—Eli's gasp for breath, his startled eyes, his warm body pressing her into the floor.

She heard herself sob. He was dead now, but he wasn't going to stay that way. She would get him back. She would have the chance to tell him that she was falling for him, too. Hard.

Her scientific brain rattled away as it processed new data. The appearance of the Voice; the undeniable connection she'd felt to him upon sight; the increase in feeling over the last few days. There could be no doubt: she'd had some kind of biological reaction to Eli.

The revelation brought more relief. She'd been worried about how quickly and easily she'd fallen for her kidnapper.

Stockholm syndrome was not sexy.

But this? This she could understand.

She pulled herself out of her thoughts. The Voice had been right; Eli was going to need her. He'd been so disoriented last time. Human touch had grounded him.

She wove her fingers back into Eli's hair, and Abilene's other hand moved to rest against Eli's bicep, and she squeezed. The image of Eli curled on his side wavered through tears collected in her eyelashes.

The skin beneath her hands continued to gain warmth, and she kept a constant vigil on the progress his wound was making in the healing process.

When the skin closed together on Eli's once-again flawless back, excitement bordering on giddiness punched through her gut.

Soon, the Voice whispered.

Abilene shifted her weight. She realized with a start that she'd missed him.

She pulled on his shoulder and watched his body settle onto his back once more. His eyes were darting around behind his eyelids.

His mouth opened, and he swallowed a huge gulp of air. She moved her hand to his face, cradling his cheek.

"Shh," she whispered. "You're okay." It was what she'd said to him the first time.

Eli's eyes opened and focused on her in an instant. Confusion marred his face.

"Eli," she said more firmly, using his name to remind him of who his was. "You're alive and safe."

His eyes snapped with comprehension. His features relaxed, and he reached for her, his arms bending at the elbows but not quite making it off of the forest floor.

Abilene met him more than halfway, nearly throwing herself on him. As his arms wrapped around her, she buried her face near his collarbone and allowed her shaking sobs to overtake her, relief leaving her body in waves of tears.

It took him a few tries, but Eli moved his hand to her hair, pulling her closer. "No, Abi," he whispered, distressed by her crying.

She knew she needed to stop, that she was supposed to be helping *him*, not the other way around, but her emotions had run away with her. She clutched him, her fingers nearly claws.Eli simply let her cry. He continued to hold her and whisper nonsense syllables to soothe her, both his arms and his voice gaining in strength.

When his hug was so tight she had trouble breathing, she was able to stem the flow of tears. She lay still until her hiccups subsided.

"I'm sorry I didn't believe you," she whispered into the damp skin beneath her cheek.

He chuckled. "You're apologizing to *me*?" he asked. "I was sure you were going to make me crawl all the way to Georgia on my knees before you forgave me."

"Shut up," she mumbled as she snuggled in even closer.

Eli sighed, the sound a mark of contentment. His hand moved beneath her chin and tilted her face up until they were nose-to-nose. "Care to make it up to me?" he asked.

"Well, don't you wake up from *dying* in a good mood," she groused, pushing him lightly in the shoulder. He grinned and rolled on top of her, settling between her thighs and pinning her with his weight.

"What can I say? I'm a freak," and he actually *winked* at her.

It was what finally got her out of the dark place she'd been residing in since realizing Eli was dead. Abilene gave up a burble of laughter. "Well, thank God for that," she said. "Your freakish nature is one of the many things I love—" Abilene trailed off.

They both froze. Eli's grin faded to a less-brilliant but softer version of happiness.

His hand moved to brush a curl behind her ear. "Truth is, darlin'," he began, "I *don't* usually wake up from dying in a good mood." He traced the edge of her ear with one finger, but his penetrating gaze never left her eyes. "I take days to recover. The fear is . . .paralyzing."

Now his hand moved to the back of her neck. He tilted her head back. "But you," he hesitated for a moment to collect the right words. "Abi, you're the light in a plane of darkness." He leaned down and brushed his lips back and forth across hers. Once. Twice.

"I hear your voice and come alive."

And then he was kissing her. These were not the desperate kisses they'd shared over the last three days. He was kissing her like a man who was savoring what he knew was his.

He worked his arms between her and the earth and cradled her like a treasure, all the while continuing the languid kisses that were bringing Abilene's blood to a very quick, very demanding boil.

She raised her knees on each side of Eli's hips, and he settled himself against the heat between her thighs as though he were coming home.

They were both breathing heavily now, their breaths echoing among the trees. Eli began to rock against her in a slow, capable rhythm, and she broke from the kiss to look into his face.

His eyes were bluer than she'd ever seen them. He wasn't smiling anymore, but the expression he wore was so full of adoration and promise that her breathing ceased.

He stilled. The connection between them thrummed with passion.

"I love you."

They'd whispered it simultaneously. Simply. As fact.

Eli's smile returned. He leaned down to kiss her again, and just before his lips reached hers, Abilene whispered, "Show me."

He stopped a hair's breadth away.

"What?" he breathed.

"Show me you love me."

It took a few beats for her words to register, but then Eli's eyes dilated in an instant. His brows met in the middle, his lips parting to emit a nearly inaudible moan.

His lips came crashing down. Abilene parted hers, and she felt Eli's arms tighten around her further.

Their eyes were still open and locked on each other. Abilene had never kissed with her eyes open before, and now she wondered why. It was the most amazing connection. She could measure the lust and desire growing in his hooded gaze with each stroke of her tongue. Each caress of her hand down his back. Each rock of his hips against her.

Her skin rippled with sensation where her chest was pressing against his. The fabric of their clothing began to prove a debilitating distraction to her. She needed to feel him.

Her hands moved to the hem of her t-shirt, and she yanked at it. He pulled away from the kiss to sit back on his heels, bringing her up with him until she was sitting. He replaced her hands with his own and brought her shirt up and over her head.

His eyes raked her breasts and belly as he spread her t-shirt on the ground behind her. Then he pushed on her shoulders until she lay back down, the shirt shielding her from the dirt beneath them. He trailed his fingers from her waist to her bra. "Off," he whispered in a rough voice, incapable of a more refined request.

Abilene arched her back from the ground and reached behind her back to unhook her bra. She lowered herself again, and then dragged the bra straps from her shoulders until she was able to lay bare to his gaze.

"Oh, Jesus," he groaned. He cupped a breast with each hand, the calluses on his palms abrading her skin. "You're so fucking perfect."

Abilene's panties were drenched for him. She needed to feel his naked chest on hers *now*. She reached up and pulled him down to her with surprising strength. His hands landed in the dirt beside her head; his fingers splayed. The moment their skin touched, they both moaned.

Every muscle in Eli's upper body was taught with control. Abilene writhed beneath him, moving her hips until he was once again pressed against her core.

"Please," she entreated, rocking her hips up and down. She was panting, and Eli was quick to follow her urging. He moved his entire body against her, rubbing against her nipples with his chest, against the apex of her thighs with his firm length.

He was breathing as frantically as she was. One of his large hands moved from its position beside her head to between their bodies as he worked at her button and fly.

"I need you so badly," he gasped. "God, I've never needed anyone this badly."

It was the same frantic idea she had roiling through her own passion-addled brain. She worked to help him get her pants off, shimmying her hips back and forth until Eli pulled them off. He maneuvered her body to place the pants beneath her in the same fashion as her shirt.

When he moved to spread atop her again, Abilene stopped him with a hand to his chest. "No," she protested, raking her nails down his abdomen, marveling as his muscles rippled in her hand's wake. "You, too." Her hand reached the waistband of his pants, and she pulled at it.

Eli's eyes came back to hers, and he gave her an evaluating look. She remembered how nervous she'd been in the hotel room last night when she'd taken his pants off for the first time. There was no nervousness now, just a frenzied need to have him naked. He seemed to see that in her eyes, for he removed his pants. Abilene didn't even have the opportunity to touch him before he was back between her thighs, his full weight resting atop her.

"Am I too heavy?" he asked.

He was lusciously heavy. "Yes," she moaned. He immediately moved back. She clutched at him. "No!" She didn't want him to move! What was he thinking?

He smiled and returned to her. "I'm getting mixed signals, darlin'," he chuckled. And then they were flush against each other, the only barrier between them Abilene's panties. The humor evaporated from Eli's face.

"Oh, Abi," he sighed. He moved against her as he had earlier, his entire body brushing hers. But now, without the numbing agent of clothing, the sensations were sharp. Beyond pleasurable.

Eli squeezed his eyes shut and rocked again. A sound of near-pain fell from his parted lips.

Abilene had never felt anything like it. Even the pleasure she'd already shared with Eli paled in comparison to the feel of lying naked beneath him. The different textures of Eli's body were a fascination to her own. The brush of Eli's legs against the inside of her thighs, the insistent erection cradled in the softness between her legs, his firm abdomen plastered against her soft stomach— she was mindless from the experiences bombarding her.

But it was the sensations at her core that were driving her insane. She began to rock with him, each thrust bringing her closer to the edge.

Abilene became aware that she was whimpering with every breath. "Don't make me wait anymore," she begged him, no longer able to withstand the torture of not knowing what it felt to have him inside her.

In seconds her panties were gone, and one of Eli's thick fingers filled her. Abilene nearly came undone on the spot. Her head kicked back; her hips rocked into his touch.

Eli began to thrust his finger slowly in and out, and when she brought her eyes back to his face, she found him watching her avidly. His cheeks were flushed, and his bottom lip was caught between his teeth.

Her body responded to the sight in a flood of moisture. Eli felt it, groaned, and filled her more completely by easing another finger inside of her.

It was too much. Abilene felt the beginning tremors of release, and just as she began to cry out, Eli removed his fingers, stopping her orgasm in its tracks.

She whimpered and opened her eyes.

"Not yet, baby," he whispered as he settled himself back between her thighs, his erection prodding her. "Wait for me."

Abilene *loved* that plan. She wiggled beneath him, and he gave a lopsided smile in response.

Abilene felt Eli's hand guiding his length to her entrance when his smile melted from his face. He started to swallow repeatedly; his eyes glazed. She kept waiting for him to move, but he couldn't seem to.

"Eli?" she asked. She moved against him again, and he stilled her with a hand to her hip.

"I don't think I can hurt you," he whispered, minimal sound accompanying the words.

Abilene closed her eyes. It was stupid, but she'd completely forgotten that she was a virgin. "Oh, yeah," she muttered.

The nervousness that had been miles away swamped Abilene, but it wasn't enough to overshadow need. She trailed her hands up

Eli's arms, across his shoulders, and around his neck. She pulled him down until their lips touched, fighting his tense muscles the entire way.

When Abilene began kissing him, Eli didn't relax one iota. It wasn't until Abilene trailed her hands down his back to rest on his ass that she got a reaction. His body seemed to respond with a mind of its own to her grasp, and his hips kicked forward. The tip of his erection penetrated her slightly, and just as quickly it was gone.

Abilene's wild moan rent the air. "*Eli . . . .*" Oh, God, he just had to do that again.

When she opened her eyes, it was to the sight of Eli's head hanging down from his shoulders, his hair brushing her breasts, his weight resting on his arms.

His entire body was shaking.

"Oh . . . honey," she trailed her fingers through his hair. "It's okay." He brought his head up to look at her with anguished eyes.

"It hurts more to be without you," she murmured to him.

She was relieved when a determined look replaced Eli's trepidation. She felt a gentle prodding, and then Eli thrust into her long and hard, pushing past the barrier of her virginity.

She couldn't help it; she cried out. Her every muscle stiffened around the invasion of Eli's body. *Ouch, ouch ouch!*

Suddenly, Eli was there, brushing frantic kisses across her cheeks, her nose, her chin. "I'm sorry," he kept whispering over and over. "God, I'm so sorry. I'll make it up to you, I promise."

She wanted to assure him that she was okay; she wanted to make him feel better. But she couldn't. It had been way more painful than she anticipated. She couldn't even catch her breath to speak.

After several moments, when the sharpness of the pain had dulled, Abilene began to unclamp the death-hold her muscles had on her bones. She was relieved when it registered that the fullness that had felt like an assault moments ago was turning into a feeling of completion. Of belonging.

All at once, it didn't feel so awful.

She moved beneath him hesitantly. Eli's length glided into her further. She sighed.

Now that was downright lovely.

Eli rested his forehead against hers.

***

Eli was devastated. It went against every instinct in his body to inflict pain upon Abilene.

And here he was, buried deeply inside her body—the place he most wanted to be—and he was staring at blue eyes brimming with unshed tears. If he didn't fix this for her, and soon, he was going to start boohooing worse than she was.

Abilene wiggled beneath him again, and, though he tried to stifle it, pleasure rocketed through him. Then she made a noise of distress.

"We'll stop," he offered desperately. "I'll stop right now." He made a move to do just that when Abilene's nails dug into his shoulders.

"To hell with that," she retorted, then followed up her statement with another movement of her hips.

Eli realized that what he had taken as a sound of distress was really a sound of frustration. Abilene had been trying to get him to move for the past few minutes, and he had been too much of an idiot to pick up on her signals.

Relief rained down on him. *She's okay. Oh, thank God, she's okay.*

He squeezed her to himself, and she squeaked, but then tried to pat him reassuringly where her hands rested. He just held her for a bit, but then Abilene cleared her throat.

"Um, shouldn't you be moving?" she asked. "Or something?"

His chuckle rumbled around in his chest as he pulled back from the death grip he had on his woman. "Yes, ma'am," he drawled, and he drew his hips back. He withdrew until he had nearly left her body, watching as her eyelids fluttered down. Then he filled her again, moving so achingly slow that the restraint was almost a physical pain.

When he was seated to the hilt again, Abilene's warm flesh clenched around him, wrenching a disbelieving moan from his now-dry mouth.

"Oh . . . God," he grunted unintelligibly through gritted teeth as he fought the urge to spill inside of her.

Abilene was proving a quick study in what pleased him, because the sensation repeated, and Eli had to bury his face in her neck and tune out all sensation to keep from ending their first lovemaking session then and there.

"You feel so good," she breathed into his ear, and Eli fought the urge to snort in disbelief. *He* felt good?

When he had himself under control again, he began a slow, thrusting rhythm. He turned his face to plant an open-mouthed kiss to the throbbing pulse in Abilene's neck, licking the spot languidly.

In response, Abilene wrapped her legs around him and dug her heels into the backs of his thighs.

"*Abi* . . .killing me," he groaned, his measured speed picking up slightly.

"*Yes*," she cried, turning her head and *biting* his ear.

Eli broke.

Both of his hands snatched her up beneath her ass, tilting her hips to accommodate his now-frenzied thrusts.

Abilene cried out again, raking her nails down his back and burying them into his backside. She matched his rhythm, rocking her hips in time with his, and ending each searing thrust with a life-altering grind against his pelvic bone.

Eli had to clamp his lips closed around the brutal yells that left his body with each movement, and they were only growing in volume the closer he brought them to release.

He'd never been a loud lover, but Abilene was turning him into an animal. He couldn't keep quiet in the onslaught of sensation and emotion she brought him.

God, he was *loving* his *woman*. He never wanted to stop, but he felt his orgasm curling at the base of his spine. He reached between them to squeeze her clit gently.

"*Soon* . . . Abi," he panted against her neck. And as soon as the words left his mouth, he felt the tremors of her release as her core convulsed around him.

He looked down at her as her arms clutched him. She cried out his name and looked straight into his eyes as she came apart in his arms.

He was right on her heels.

He threw his head back at the force of his ejaculation and bellowed to the sky. He came in waves and waves, his breath coming in short bursts, his chest billowing in and out.

It had *never* felt like this—this strong, this perfect, this special—in his life. The connection he felt to Abilene in this moment was almost spiritual in its power.

When he was able to entertain complex thought again, he turned onto his side, bringing Abilene with him. He stayed inside her as he kissed her lips tenderly.

Her breathing mingled with his as both of their heart rates slowed. When Eli tasted salt, he pulled away in alarm. There were tear tracks on Abilene's face.

Before Eli had the chance to panic, she kissed him again. "I didn't know it would be like that," she whispered against his lips.

Eli relaxed and drew her in closer. "I love you," he murmured between kisses. The emotion swelled so profoundly in his chest that he felt the prick of tears in his own eyes.

He began to harden again, and Abilene pulled back to look at him in surprise. She smiled. "As your doctor," she began, "I feel it necessary to tell you that's not normal."

He deepened their kiss and rolled them over again until he was on his back, and Abilene was straddling his hips. Her eyes darkened with desire at the new angle of his penetration, and she rose up on her knees before easing back down.

Eli gasped. "It's normal for me when I'm around you."

Abilene grinned, and then proceeded to ensure he didn't speak coherently again for some time.

Chapter Fourteen

Abilene brushed her fingers back and forth across her swollen lips. To say that her life had changed in the last few hours would be the understatement of the century.

She was in love.

It was a pretty incredible feeling. Here, snuggled up beneath Eli's arm in the middle of the truck, she felt the safest she'd ever been.

Eli was driving with one arm over the top of the steering wheel. The other was wrapped around Abilene's shoulder. He held her in the curve of his body and was rubbing his hand up and down her arm.

It was the careless contact of a couple comfortable in a relationship, and it was something Abilene had never experienced.

It was kind of freaking her out.

Eli was behaving so *normally* when the last few hours had been anything but normal. He'd *died*. Then he'd come back to life. They'd confessed their love for each other, and then had earth-bending, mind-altering sex.

Quite frankly, she wished *he* were freaking out so she wouldn't feel so bad about doing so herself.

Oh, she didn't regret a second of it. In fact, she was already eyeing Eli askance, hoping they could make love again soon.

That shit was addictive.

But that didn't mean it wasn't a lot of changes in a short amount of time.

When things changed, Abilene screwed up. It was just a fact of life. Like the sun rising in the East or winter following autumn, this was a fact of nature. If something were new or different, Abilene would find a way to ruin it.

And embarrass those she cared about in the process.

Images of her parents appeared before her eyes. *You have to be perfect. We expect you to be perfect. Perfect, perfect, perfect.*

The thought of looking into Eli's face and seeing the disappointment she saw in her parents' eyes over and over again was nearly debilitating.

Eli's voice pulled her from her revelry.

"What has you frowning, darlin'?" he drawled.

She raised her eyes and put forth her best effort in trying to smile for him, but could tell it was unimpressive when Eli continued to look concerned.

Rather than try to answer she leaned over to nuzzle his neck. It worked better than she could have ever guessed.

Eli's body jolted against her, and seconds later, the sound of the tires on gravel announced that Eli had steered the truck to the shoulder.

In the next breath, Eli had Abilene pressed against the bench seat and was settling himself between her thighs.

With a happy sigh, Abilene wrapped her arms around Eli's neck and met him halfway for a deep kiss.

When they were like this, Abilene had no reason to doubt. They were so good together.

She reached between them to unbutton Eli's pants, and was surprised when Eli's hand stopped her own. His mouth moved to her ear, his shortened breaths puffing against her skin.

"You've gotta be sore, baby," he protested when Abilene tried to go for his jeans' button again.

She shook her head in denial, but he continued to hold her hand still while placing tantalizing kisses along the column of her neck.

Oh, hell, no was he going to stoke the fire and deny her the pay-off.She arched her back, thrusting her breasts into his chest. She felt his breath hitch and turned her head to take his earlobe between her teeth.

He growled. "Abi," he warned.

She felt the thrill of control. It was one of the first times in her life she had felt powerful. No way was she going to back off.

"I want you," she whispered into his hair. "Are you really going to deny me?" Her voice a purr, and she could feel it vibrate through Eli's body as he shivered.

He groaned in defeat and released her hand.

In no time at all, Abilene had his pants open and her hand wrapped around the velvety hardness of Eli's erection. His breathing had resumed its shortened, panting pattern, and he seemed unable to keep from thrusting into her grip.

"Do you feel what you do to me?" he mumbled through the grittiness of desire. He gathered her into his arms.

She adored how he surrounded her when they made love, pulling her to him as closely as possible, his arms between her and the seat.

She opened her own pants, and he helped her maneuver her jeans and panties down her thighs, over her knees, and off her legs altogether.

It was cramped quarters in the cab of the truck, but she didn't notice the discomfort as Eli positioned himself at her opening and gently entered her in one measured stroke.

When he was fully seated inside of her, they both moaned and froze at the onslaught of sensation.

Eli's eyes brimmed with emotion as he looked into her face, their noses brushing. "You're so beautiful, Abi," he breathed as he withdrew and slide back into her.

She leaned up and sucked his lower lip between her teeth. Eli closed his eyes and groaned as she snaked her tongue into his mouth.

As he continued to move in her, he whispered how he loved her in a constant mantra, the words ratcheting up her pleasure until her orgasm took them both by surprise, pouring through her and taking him right along with her.

Eli continued to hold her tightly as they caught their breath. "I didn't hurt you, did I?" he whispered.

She shook her head and tightened her own hold. "Not even close," she whispered back.

"We need to keep driving," Eli groaned several minutes later, "but I don't want to move."

Abilene smiled towards the ceiling of the cab. "We can always stop again if we need to."

He chuckled, the sound reverberating through her chest. "God, could you be any more perfect?"

The marrow froze in Abilene's bones.

She had begun to push on Eli's chest without realizing it until Eli captured her hands in one of his own.

"Whoa, Abi," he said quickly, an edge of worry to his tone. "Are you sure I didn't hurt you?"

You did! her mind screamed. How had that filthy word found its way into Eli's association with her?

She struggled against the hold Eli had on her. "I'm not perfect," she said.

When Eli chuckled and breathed a delighted, "Sure you are," she pinned him with a glare. His smile slipped from his face like an egg from a plate. In its wake, his brows merged together, and his lips parted in bewilderment.

"Okaaay," Eli said, drawing the word out for several syllables.

Eli moved from on top of her, but tried to keep her within his arms. When she moved out of his embrace and across the cab, Eli frowned further.

Hell, she knew she was overreacting. Eli had no idea how her perfection—or, rather, lack thereof—had been tossed into her face her entire life.

But, to throw this on top of the rapidly increasing shit pile that consisted of the last three days . . . .

She faked the best smile she could. "Shouldn't we be going?" she asked as calmly as she could.

"Abi, did I—"

She cut him off by reaching across the cab to take his hand in hers. The last thing she wanted to do right now was to have this conversation. "Sorry," she began, working to find an excuse he would believe. "I know I'm freaking out on you. God knows what my hormones are up to with all this," she paused to gesture between the two of them with her free hand, "going on between us. I'm fine. "

I'm not! some ten-year-old version of herself howled from the corner of her mind.

He still looked at her suspiciously, but either because they really did need to get moving or because she was an excellent actress, he turned to the steering wheel, putting his pants back into order.

He gave her a wolfish grin, one side of his mouth kicking up further than the other, but it lacked some of its former luster. "You're going to have to put something on if you want me to focus on anything other than you."

She blushed, and picked her pants and underwear from the floorboards and slipped them on as Eli steered the truck onto the freeway.

Perfect, perfect, perfect. . . .

He thought she was perfect.

Panic bubbled up in her throat. Oh God, she hadn't escaped at all. She'd left her parents to break away from their heavy-handed ways, their efforts to make her perfect, only to land with another someone who wanted her to be perfect.

I love you, he'd told her over and over in the last few hours, varying degrees of passion tinting the words in a different light each time.

Her heart flipped in her chest. Sure he did.

He loved *perfect* Abilene. What about when she wasn't perfect? When would someone love *her*?

Chapter Fifteen

As Eli turned the truck onto the hidden driveway of Sergeant Collins' house, he looked at Abilene's profile for the thousandth time and wondered once more what he had done to turn her so cold.

I had been a very long drive to Atlanta with her refusing to talk to him and with him constantly hiding the reaction his body had to her within a confined space.

Jeez, if he'd thought having Abilene would be a satiating scratch to an itch, he now knew how mistaken that notion was. If anything, he was *more* aware of her. All it took was the rustle of her clothing as she breathed, a waft of her sent across the truck, the slow crossing of her legs, and he would be as hard as granite.

Hell, maybe *that* was why she wasn't talking to him. Three times was a bit much for a virgin.

He cursed himself.

He'd *known* he shouldn't have let things get out of hand that last time. But had that stopped him from plowing into her sweet heat?

He had to get a handle on whatever kind of animal his body was turning him into with regards to Abilene before he hurt her, or worse, drove her away.

The silhouette of Collins's two-story plantation-style house now loomed in front of the truck, and Eli felt the quickening of nervousness in his stomach.

It had been eight years.

What if Collins didn't live here anymore?

What if he didn't care what had happened to Eli?

Or, God, what if he was somehow involved?

He *had* encouraged Eli to join the Berets. Had that been part of some plan?

His mother's philosophy on trust reared its head once again. Involuntarily, he turned his head to look at Abilene in the quietness of the cab.

Past betrayals bombarded him.

His father.

Major Taylor.

Sergeant Collins?

He shivered as his mind made the natural trip to the next person on the list.

Abilene?

He slammed on the breaks causing his tires to squeal on the drive.

No! he shouted at himself. You will *not* go down this path.

His father and Major Taylor were bad people. Sergeant was nothing like them. And Abilene. . . .

She wouldn't.

Would she?

This isn't helping, the Voice scolded.

Right. He nodded his head. *No more of that line of thought.* He jumped when Abilene broke her silence.

"Where are we?" she whispered into the dark. Her voice wavered. Eli reached for her hand.

"A friend's house," he reassured her, squeezing her hand. "He'll help us."

Eli hoped.

Abilene moved to open her door, but Eli tugged on her hand. "Wait for me," he admonished her, exiting the truck and walking around the front to her door. "You're going to have to get used to this," he told her as he opened her door and offered her a hand down.

Some of the uncomfortable tension between them eased as Abilene gave him her first genuine smile since they'd last spoken.

"I could definitely get used to it," she replied. Before she could object, he swooped in to brush a quick kiss across her lips.

"Good."

With her hand grasped in his, Eli began a noisy trek up to Collins' front door. Whoever lived here, he didn't want to sneak up on them in the middle of the night. This was the South after all, and—

The sound of a shotgun being pumped rent the night.

Eli stopped in his tracks, shoved a gasping Abilene behind him, and stared into the hallow black eye of a deadly Winchester.

Despite the intensity of a gun in the face, Eli let out a breath of air in relief.

From one look, Eli knew the gun was not civilian issue.

Sergeant Collins still lived here.

Eli had found him.

Granted, Collins was now holding Eli and the woman Eli cared for more than his own life at gunpoint. But one had to claim victory where one could.

"Stay right where ya are, and don't try anything funny." The voice saying those words was so distorted through Southern twang that it was almost comical. But Eli knew Collins to be a formidable opponent, and the gun he wielded would do some serious damage to Eli. Unlike the weapon Major Taylor had used, a slug from a Winchester would go right through him and plow into Abilene before it was spent.

Not an option.

"Sarge?" Eli asked.

The barrel of the shotgun wavered. "Who's there?" Collins barked.

"It's Eli."

Several beats of silence.

"Eli?" Sergeant Collins voice dripped with an unidentifiable emotion. Something between hope and disbelief.

"Yes, sir. Eli Johnson."

Eli heard Collins fumble around in the dark. A second later there was a click, and a powerful light shone in his eyes.

Eli raised a hand to stem the glare, but forced it back down again, affording Collins a clear look at his face: a face Eli knew hadn't changed in the near-decade since Sergeant Collins had last seen him.

"Oh, shit," Collins murmured.

Abilene must have determined that the aging Sergeant was no threat because she poked her head over Eli's shoulder to look at him.

Sergeant Collins saw her and cleared his throat. "Whoa, pardon my language, ma'am. Didn't see you there."

The presence of a lady had Collins dropping the barrel of his shotgun as well as the beam of his flashlight so that they both pointed to the dirt beside his feet.

In the relative darkness, Eli was able to make out the features of the man who was more father than friend.

The two men stared at each other.

When the Sergeant continued to clear his throat for a few moments, Eli was confused, until it became obvious that his mentor was fighting against tears.

When Collins lost the battle and two beads of emotion slipped from his lids to travel down the timeworn cheeks of his face, Eli strode forward.

He reached the older man in two steps, but then stalled out.

What was the appropriate action here? Should Eli shake his hand? No, that didn't seem right.

All of this work to get here, face-to-face with this man, and Eli didn't know what to do.

"Hey," Eli blurted.

Sergeant Collins leaned down toward the right, his knees emitting creaks and cracks, to place his shotgun on the ground. Then, with the speed of a much younger man, he snapped upright again and gathered Eli into a bone-crushing hug.

Eli froze for only a second—surprised at the panic that accompanied being touched—until he realized that this was Sarge.

This was what Eli should have done when he'd stepped toward the man.

Eli brought his arms up to return the man's embrace. They held on to each other for several seconds before Sergeant Collins beat Eli on the back a couple of times and released him.

"Thought you were dead," Collins grunted while scrubbing two gnarled hands against his eyes.

Only every once in a while.

"No," Eli said instead.

Collins gazed at Abilene with watery eyes, and Eli turned toward her to make introductions. "This is Abilene," he began. "My—" He drifted off. *Woman* had been on the tip of his tongue. That wouldn't have earned him any points.

"Friend," Abilene finished for him as she stepped forward to take Collins's hand in her own.

Eli frowned at her narrow back.

Friend, hell.

They were going to have to have a Come-to-Jesus meeting if she thought she was Eli's *friend.*

"You kids come on into the house," Collins grumbled. "We can't be standing out here in the dark like a bunch of wide-eyed idjiots."

"Yes, sir," Eli answered automatically, his hand falling to the small of Abilene's back as they followed Sergeant Collins to the front door.

Her muscles bunched and released beneath his palm, and Eli forced his thoughts to other things before he could ponder how soon he would be able to get Abilene alone again.

Inside the house, Sergeant Collins propped his gun against the doorframe and clicked on the lights as he made his way into the kitchen.

He gestured for Abilene and Eli to sit at the kitchen table, and then he moved to the refrigerator and disappeared inside.

Eli took this time to reacquaint himself with Sergeant Collins' kitchen. It looked almost identical to the kitchen Eli remembered from the past: traditional, country wallpaper with geese printed in a border around the top; dull, wooden countertops; out-dated white appliances; rickety, oak table. It held the same charming appeal that had always shocked Eli as a young recruit. Sergeant Collins was gritty and rough around the edges, but his house reflected a care for comfort and home that few knew the Sergeant had in him.

Eli noticed a few new additions to the décor. Lace curtains. A display of dishes on the wall.

Feminine touches.

Eli looked at where Sergeant Collins was emerging from the fridge, wondering if the man had found love in the last eight years.

Eli hoped so. If anyone deserved happiness, it was Sarge.

Sergeant Collins made his way toward the table, a jug of milk with three stacked cups turned over and balanced on top of the spout in one hand, and a package of Oreos in the other.

Abilene rose to help him, taking the Oreos so he could grab the cups before they fell, and Eli dimly thought that he should have done that instead. But he was incapable of movement.

Here, in the bright florescent light, Eli could see Sergeant Collins clearly for the first time.

And it was a shock.

Collins' jet-black hair was now overrun with grey. It started at his temples, then feathered back and all throughout. His commanding face was soft around the edges, his firm jaw gone. The Sergeant's once-tan skin held a sallow tint, but there were two bright pink points of excitement in his cheeks and glints of pleasure in dark green eyes that had obviously had few reasons to smile in recent history.

He looked . . .old. Not just age-old, but soul-old. As though life had been kicking him when he was down, and the fight had been beaten out of him.

Eli thought sadly that he might have had something to do with Sergeant Collins' current aura of sadness, though he hoped that wasn't the case.

Collins sat the milk on the table and sank into the chair to Eli's right with a sigh. He put his hand on Eli's shoulder, and the tiny happiness in his eyes flared for a second.

"Still can't believe you're here," he said.

Eli reached up to give his hand a squeeze, and it seemed to jerk Collins from his inward thoughts.

The Sergeant cleared his throat. "So, *why* are you here, son?" he asked. "And *how*? Your mama and I were told you were dead."

Eli nodded, wondering for a moment at the mention of his mother and his mentor as a collective unit. "Well, I have been." Sergeant Collins' eyes narrowed. "Dead," Eli clarified. "Several times," Eli finished, as though it weren't the big deal that it was.

The air of the kitchen filled with tension. It caused the hair on Eli's arms to stand up. Collins' face twisted into a glower.

"Don't tell me those fool-rumors are true," Collins growled.

Rumors. Eli's heart leapt at the word. It meant, perhaps, that he had not been forgotten; that at least a portion of the Tormentor's treachery had escaped his tight hold on the truth.

"What rumors?" Abilene asked, not content to view this conversation from the sidelines.

"That the key to immortality had been unlocked," Sergeant Collins scoffed. "That they had found a way to create a death-proof soldier."

Abilene scrunched her brow. "People were saying that?" she asked. "I just went through medical school; no one ever mentioned this—in print or in person."

"No, you wouldn't have heard anything," Collins said, shaking his head. "You're a civilian. These rumors circulated among a very small, very select group of government intelligence agents." Collins shrugged. "*I* only know because I beat down doors and called in favors when Eli's mother—" A guilty flush colored the Sergeant's face.

Eli straightened. This was the second time Sergeant Collins had mentioned Eli's mother.

"What about my mother, Sarge?" Eli asked.

Sergeant Collins screwed his mouth down into a frown, then met Eli's eyes. "Hell, boy, you know I . . .*loved*," here Collins squirmed, "you like a son."

Something tingled at the back of Eli's neck. The words were wonderful, but something in the Sergeant's tone caused Eli alarm.

"Well, when you disappeared," Collins continued, "your mama came to me for help. She didn't buy your *Killed in Action* status, nor should she have." Collins emitted a deep chuckle. "She's a smart cookie, your mama. They wouldn't release your body. She pitched a royal fit, claiming they were hiding something from her. That if you had died, they needed to send you home so she could bury you properly."

Sergeant Collins paused in his story and looked down into his lap where his hands were knotted together. "One look at her, and I was a goner," he revealed. "She was so full of passion. So full of loyalty to you—which was something we had in common."

"I married her, son," Sergeant Collins finished in a whisper.

Happiness flooded Eli. It was almost too good to be true. "Married her?" Eli repeated. God, someone had been here to take care of his mother while Eli was gone. He was so grateful to his mentor that he was tempted to give him a huge ole kiss.

And then Eli realized something. If Sarge had married her, she was here. In his house!

Eli surged to his feet; his chair screeched on the floor as it shot back. "Where is she?" He was charging toward the door before Collins could answer.

"Hold on now, son," the Sergeant called to Eli's back. It didn't even begin to slow Eli down. He stepped into the doorframe so he could look up and down the hall. He was determined to find his mama one way or the other, even if he had to open every door in the house.

"Eli, stop!" Sergeant Collins barked. Eli halted.

That was a command from his superior officer.

Eli turned around. The niggling feeling of worry was back, lodged at the base of Eli's brain.

"Where is she?" Eli repeated.

"I found out about Operation: Middle of the Garden, Eli."

It was the one thing the man could have said to diffuse the situation. Eli visibly crumbled, though he still stood. Sergeant Collins walked around the table, his hands held out in a pose of supplication.

"I promised your mama I would get to the bottom of what had happened to you. Your disappearance was very suspicious. It reeked of a cover-up. I was able to pinpoint your last known location, but no one—not any soldiers from your unit, not any officers—would admit to knowing how you had died. They simply said you were there one day and gone the next.

"That's when I started pounding the pavement. I called in every favor I had, followed every lead. I heard the rumors about the immortal soldier and that they were testing men in a top-secret government operation."

Eli made an involuntary noise of distress. Collins heard it and swore under his breath.

Abilene left her chair and moved to Eli's side. She took his hand in between her own and cradled it against her stomach. He spared her a quick, grateful glace, then returned his attention to Sergeant Collins.

"I found out you were involved in the operation. Operation: Middle of the Garden was an embarrassment; a blight on the reputation of the United States Army. When word was leaked that scientists were conducting experiments on civilians, the entire program was shut down. I was given access to your files."

Sergeant Collins gaze turned imploring. "Your death was recorded in vivid detail, Eli. I finally believed that you were dead. I couldn't tell your mother what had really happened to you. She was sick. Fragile."

Eli grunted. He knew that. It had been the only reason he had agreed to be a test subject: so his mother would be supported.

"So, I just told her that the Army's initial report on your death was true."

Eli sighed with relief. Sergeant Collins had made the right decision. God, the thought of his mother knowing what he had gone through—

"But, she gave up," Collins whispered. He pulled in a ragged breath that caused his chest to buck up and down. "She knew it wasn't true, that I had lied to her. It broke her, ruined us, and caused her to stop fighting the disease."

"Where . . .is . . .she?" Eli enunciated through clenched teeth.

Sergeant Collins swallowed several times and looked at his feet. "She passed."

The walls of the kitchen closed in on Eli until he couldn't breathe. Spots danced in front of his eyes. He felt Abilene put her arm around him and guide him back to the chair he had vacated earlier.

When she tried to force his head between his knees, he snapped.

"No!" he yelled, swiping his arm out to the side in a cutting motion, sending Abilene scurrying back.

Eli noticed that Sergeant Collins had made his way back to the table himself. The man looked as though he had aged even more in the last few minutes. His eyes were dark.

Conflicting emotions warred within Eli. The Sergeant had done exactly what Eli would have: protected Eli's mother from the devastating truth of what had happened to him.

Yet, Eli felt anger as well. Of course his mother would have shut down if she suspected Collins of lying. Trust was so hard for her in the first place. If she had suspected her second husband of being the same kind of man as her first. . . .

Eli groaned aloud and allowed Abilene to push his head down until he was looking at the tiled floor from between his knees.

His mother died unhappy.

And it was Eli's fault.

The slight weight of Abilene's hand landed between Eli's shoulder blades. She began a soothing, circular motion that encompassed his entire back, and Eli felt his muscles relent their death grip on his bones.

Eli sighed.

"Eli, God, I'm so sorry, son." Sergeant Collins huffed out a breath and plowed his stubby fingers through his hair. "There's just no delicate way to deliver news like that. I wouldn't hurt you for the world. I hope you know that."

Eli lifted his head and leveled his gaze on the worry-glazed eyes of the Sergeant. "I know." He swallowed once. Twice. Gathered his courage. "Did she suf—um, was it bad? You know, at the end?"

Sergeant Collins looked at him. Eli could see the answer in his eyes, but knew the man would never confirm Eli's worst fears.

Eli nodded. Message received.

The sharp stabbing pains of tears pricked his eyes. Eli let his head sink down again.

He was a failure.

He'd taken on the role of becoming a test subject so his mother would be okay. She'd needed the money that Eli was promised would come her way with his cooperation.

Instead of helping her, he'd ensured her painful death.

He should have died before ever allowing himself to be defiled in such a way.

And now, he never would.

The chair to his left screeched against the tile as Sergeant Collins pulled it out and fell into its support.

"Eli . . . I need to know what happened." The Sergeant paused for a moment, waiting to see how his words would be received. "You obviously escaped. You're still alive." He scooted closer to Eli and laid a hand on Eli's shoulder. "What happened in the last eight years?"

Eli spoke to the floor, his head too heavy to lift. "It's all true, Sarge. Every bit. They experimented on me. Made me eat the damned fruit. Then, when they found out it had made me immortal, they killed me. Dozens of times. And recorded my body's reaction." Eli's voice was deadpan. He relayed the information without any inflection, without any bid for pity.

Sergeant Collins sucked in a breath and absorbed the information. He must have already suspected what had happened, though, because he recovered to ask, "But how? Eli, I swear to you, I tore apart Washington trying to find you. The record of your death was very detailed and complete. I watched as they dismantled Operation: Middle of the Garden and forever put to bed the idea of experimentation. It was over. Done."

Eli shook his head and laughed without humor. "Done for who, Sarge? Not for me. I know I was moved at least once. And when I got out, I discovered I had been kept in the basement of a civilian hospital. But I was still definitely there. And Major Taylor was still experimenting on me."

When Sergeant Collins heard Major Taylor's name, he made a threatening noise in the back of his throat. "Shit, I knew that son of a bitch was trouble," he whispered. Then he remembered Abilene sat on the other side of Eli. "Excuse me, ma'am."

Abilene rolled her eyes at this. "Sure. Why the fuck not."

Some of the tension dissipated from the kitchen. Sergeant Collins let out a hearty chuckle and slapped Eli on the back as though to say job well-done. "I like her."

Me too, both his mind and the Voice chimed in.

Abilene's eyes sparkled with mischief at the compliment, and the corner of her lips tweaked up in a secret smile.

Heat rushed to his groin. It was the same smile she wore after coming apart beautifully beneath him. And above him. And—

Eli cleared his throat. "Um, Sarge, I don't suppose you can put us up for the night? I think Abilene must be tired."

The "tired" woman let out an unfeminine snort, and Sergeant Collins chuckled.

And Eli blushed.

"Sure, son, you can stay here for as long as you'd like." Then he wagged a finger in Eli's face. "But in the morning, you're telling me everything." A gleam entered the Sergeant's eyes. "And then we're going to bring the world crumbling down on Taylor's shoulders."

The words choked Eli up. They meant he wasn't alone. Wasn't fighting his own battles. That someone else recognized Eli had been wronged.

Eli recognized the same feelings shimmering in the face of the other man. Sergeant Collins clapped Eli on the back once again. "Damn glad you're here, boy," he choked out. Then he turned and led the way out of the kitchen before the men started crying like kids in front of Abilene.

***

When Sergeant Collins delivered them to the guest room, Eli stepped inside and turned to face her. He was just out of Sergeant Collins' field of vision, so only Abilene saw as Eli bit his bottom lip and trailed his eyes over her body.

Then his gaze flicked to the bed and back to her.

Holy fraking cow. Her belly quivered, and she was ready to sprint into the room and close the door behind her.

But Collins spoke. "Abilene, hon, I know Eli's mama always hated to wear clothes for too long. Do you want to look through her things before bed? See if you can find anything that would work for you?"

The tantalizing thought drove all others from her head. "God, yes. Sir," she added quickly. "That'd be great."

Clean clothes. She could feel human again.

She looked to Eli to tell him she'd be back in just a minute, but the look of disappointment on his face almost had her laughing out loud.

He looked like a kid whose favorite toy had been poached by the neighborhood bully.

"Eli, some of your old things are in boxes in the closet. And there should be soap in the shower. I'll send her back soon. I promise," Sergeant Collins teased.

Collins laid a hand in the small of her back and ushered her down the hallway to the master bedroom.

She'd just met the man, and it wasn't under the best of circumstances, but she was already a little taken with him. He just exuded a sense of concern and care. It felt so good it made Abilene dizzy.

Her own father had never cared for her.

Of course, it didn't hurt that Sergeant Collins had announced he liked her. Obviously the man had impeccable taste, and therefore had passed the "I'm okay" test with flying colors.

He escorted her to the closet of the master bedroom, announced "Help yourself, hon," and settled himself in an overstuffed armchair to watch her sift through his wife's belongings.

She began to do so, hesitantly at first—after all, it was a little intimidating to be going through the belongings of a woman who hung the moon for Eli and Collins—but Sergeant Collins kept up a steady stream of small talk. He asked about her schooling, her background. He seemed genuinely interested in her.

Soon, Abilene had a small pile of clothes hanging over one arm, and she felt comfortable enough around the man to ask a question of her own.

"Did you know Major Taylor, Mr. Collins?" She nibbled on her lip when Collins eyes darkened and snapped with emotion.

"Yes. Yes, I did."

"Eli says—do you think Major Taylor is just obsessed with the experiment and that's why he's—he did what he did to Eli? Or—"

He stepped toward her until they were face to face. "Let me put it this way. I wouldn't want him around you, or Eli's mama, or any other woman I cared about." He'd said the words firmly, but softened their message by leaning forward and giving her a kiss on her forehead.

"And it looks like we're practically family, hon, so you can call me Earl," he continued, his tone now jovial. "Now get on back to Eli before he blows a gasket."

He gave her a gentle shove in the direction of the bedroom door.

Abilene moved on legs that felt like wood. She hadn't heard a thing since Sergeant Collins announced that Taylor was dangerous to women.

She was too eaten up by guilt to do anything but obsess over something she'd managed to forget in the last three days.

Dahlia.

And Olive, and Mary, and Lisa.

But mostly Dahlia.

Major Taylor could be headed back to them right now. He could hurt them. Torture them like he'd tortured Eli.

Bile rose in her throat.

She spotted a telephone on a stand in the hallway and dove toward it.

She had to warn them. Her fingers moved over the numbers, dialing the hospital's line from memory.

If something happened to those women and Abilene didn't warn them, it would be her fault. All—

"Needles Military Hospital, how can I help you?"

The sound of Dahlia's voice rolled through her. Relief caused her to sag against the wall.

"Dahlia, thank God," Abilene sighed.

"Abi!" the other woman screeched into the phone. "Where the hell are you? Are you okay? Are you hurt? I'm gonna kick your ass!" Dahlia's words tumbled over each other, and despite the reason behind Abilene's call, she felt a bubble of laughter building in her chest.

God, how could she have forgotten about Dahlia? She deserved to have her ass kicked.

"I'm fine, I promise," she assured her friend. "But I need to tell you something very important."

There was silence on the other line for a few moments. Finally, "Fine, I'm honestly so relieved you're okay that you could tell me anything you wanted. Just know that you're in trouble. The next time I see you—"

But Abilene cut her off. She had an uneasy feeling in her stomach for a moment. Almost as though her body were telling her that she was making a mistake, though, what that mistake could be, Abilene had no idea.

"You need to be careful around Major Taylor, Dahlia," Abilene said. "He's not there, is he?"

More silence. "No," Dahlia said, "he's not here. Why do I need to be careful around Major Taylor, Abilene?"

"Never mind that," Abilene said. "Just promise me, Dahlia. Promise me you'll be careful around him. In fact," she sped up as an idea occurred to her, "leave the facility. Just take the other women and leave. Don't come back until you hear from me."

"Abilene, you're being crazy—"

"Just do it!" Abilene shouted into the phone. "Please," she finished gently.

There were several seconds of silence on the phone now. Abilene knew she'd crossed some boundaries of friendship with the way she'd yelled, but right now she just couldn't bring herself to care.

"If I promise to leave, will you at least tell me you're safe, too?" Dahlia asked.

Abilene sighed. "I'm safe. I'm in Georgia. A long, long way from trouble, I promise you."

She hoped.

She could hear Dahlia's capitulation in the way she sighed on the phone. "Alright, Abi, you win. I'll take the girls, and we'll go to Vegas or something. I can't tell them the crazy crap you just threw around, but I promise I'll find a way to get them out. Satisfied?"

Abilene looked up at the ceiling, waiting for the relief to return. It didn't. She frowned. "Yeah," she lied into the phone. "I'm satisfied."

The phone clicked in her ear.

Abilene stared down at the receiver in her hand as the dial tone filled the hallway.

She couldn't shake the feeling that she was never going to see her friend again.

Chapter Sixteen

Dahlia pressed end on her cell phone. There was no denying it: she was a genius. She'd had the facility's calls forwarded to her cell on a hunch. Thank God it had paid off.

Major Taylor eyed her from the chair he'd been sitting in through Dahlia's conversation with Abilene. His eyes were dazed from the painkillers he'd taken to ward off the agony of his injury.

Painkillers made you dull. Dahlia would have never taken them at such a critical time, but, then, she was learning that Major Taylor was proving to be a disappointment in several categories. Why not add this one to the list as well?

His arm was in a makeshift splint and sling for the moment. Dahlia had re-set the arm and stitched the wound. There was simply no time for the operation he needed. He would have to wait.

"She's in Georgia," Dahlia said. "All we have to do is find them."

Major Taylor's nostril's flared. "It's as I hoped."

Dahlia just prevented herself from verbally castrating the man. *As he'd hoped?* Her mind scoffed. *Nothing* had gone according to plan in this fiasco. *Let the man have his fantasy*, Dahlia told herself.

"Sergeant Collins lives here in Atlanta," he continued. "He was a sort of a father figure to the subject. They must be there. At his house."

He looked at her expectantly.

Oh, Christ. She was going to have to do everything, wasn't she?

She plucked the message pad and pen from the nightstand and placed them beside Major Taylor. "Address."

So, it was up to her to bring Abilene in. Fine by her. At least if she did it herself, she knew it would be done right.

Dahlia never failed.

***

When Abilene entered the guest room, Eli was nowhere to be seen. She heard the sound of the shower in the bathroom, and all of the heat from their earlier brief exchange came rushing back. Moisture pooled between her legs.

Her man was in that shower.

Naked.

She ditched the clothes on the bed and made her way into the bathroom, shedding what she wore along the way.

In the steam-filled bathroom, Eli made not a peep from the other side of the curtain. Abilene drew the curtain back.

Her heart broke.

Eli was standing under the stream of water. His back was to her. Both of his hands were braced against the tile above his head, which dipped down until his chin almost touched his chest.

His shoulders shook with silent sobs.

"Oh, Eli," she whispered.

She stepped into the tub, pressed herself against his back, and wound her arms around his waist.

He stiffened for a second. She could feel him trying to pull himself back together, but then she pressed a soft kiss to the skin of his back, and his muscles relaxed.

"She's gone," he whispered into the tile.

Her arms tightened around his middle. Her hands splayed over his abdomen and chest. "I know, baby."

"It's my fault."

Abilene's head whipped up. "No."

Eli was shaking his head, so she repeated herself. "No. Don't you dare believe that, Eli Johnson." She recognized the anger in her own voice, but could do nothing to stop it.

She'd be damned if he started blaming himself for this. It was what she'd had forced on her by her parents time and time again growing up: blame for something out of her control. She cared too much about this man to allow the same thing to happen to him.

The anger in her voice caught his attention, and he turned around to face her. His face was devastated. His eyes were red around the edges; deep lines marred his mouth.

Abilene felt her anger leech away. She brought her hand to his cheek and smoothed away the lines with her thumb until his mouth relaxed. She stood on tiptoe and pressed a kiss to his lips.

She sank back on her heels and looked him dead in the eye. "This is not your fault, sweetie. She *loved* you." Eli's eyes closed in pain. Abilene brought her other hand up to his face. She now cradled his head between both of her hands. He opened his eyes. "She loved you," Abilene repeated. "She would never want you to blame yourself for this. She would want you to honor her. To remember her." She gentled her voice. "There's no honor in blame, Eli."

She could tell he wanted to believe her, but he just wasn't there yet. So, she'd failed to comfort him that way.

There were other ways to bring him comfort.

She stepped into the warmth of his body. As soon as their chests touched, her nipples abraded by the smattering of hair on Eli's torso, Eli's eyes dilated; his pupils ate up his irises.

He breathed her name before gathering her into his arms and pulling her flush against him.

Her breath left her in a whoosh, but not from the tight hold he had on her. The heat that accompanied their close proximity always took her breath away.

He looked into her eyes as he lowered his head to press his lips to hers. His kiss was unhurried and thorough.

When her nails dug into his scalp, he gripped her ass and hauled her up. She wrapped her legs around his waist, and he walked forward until her back was pressed against the tile.

The tip of his erection was rubbing against her just where she needed him, and she squirmed to increase the friction.

"Oh, yeah, darlin'," Eli panted. "Keep doin' that."

God, she loved that his accent came out even more when they were together like this. It was one way she could tell his control was slipping.

As she continued her movement, Eli pulled back from her to trail his fingers over her collarbone and down to cup one of her breasts with his hand.

He squeezed her, and her head fell back against the tile with a thud.

"Haven't paid enough attention to these," Eli murmured, giving her nipple a gentle squeeze. It pearled instantly.

They groaned together.

"*God*, Abi . . .what you do to me."

She needed him inside her. She changed her squirming until the tip of his erection eased into her.

Eli's breath caught, and he thrust the rest of the way inside her until they were pressed as tightly together as they could be.

He was seated more deeply inside of her than he'd ever been.

The connection between them thickened. Became more than just physical. She could see it in Eli's eyes, which were shiny again.

"I love you, Abilene," he whispered. His lips were a hair's breadth from her own.

Rather than joy, she felt a pang. The word *perfect* was still in the forefront of her mind. Nevertheless, "I love you, too."

She did. So much. Which is why it hurt so much to have him love something she was not.

He ground against her, and the friction against her clit had her eyes rolling back in her head. All of the complicated thoughts fled her brain.

She just needed him.

"You're so beautiful when I make love to you," he whispered into her ear. Then he pressed several kisses along the column of her neck. When he reached her shoulder, he bit her gently.

She moaned and scraped her nails down his back.

He reached between them to rub circles around her clit with his thumb. At the same time, he set a slow steady pace, withdrawing and thrusting.

In no time at all he had her spiraling up to the breaking point. Her breaths were coming short and fast.

"Let go, baby." Eli's voice was strained now. His own ragged breathing fanned her face. "Let me watch you come apart."

He tweaked her clit, and she exploded.

He cut off her cry by covering her mouth with his, swallowing the noise she was making. But then he was groaning into *her* mouth as they reached their peaks together.

Stars exploded behind her eyes. She clutched Eli to her, knew she was digging her nails into his flesh, but couldn't temper her response to him.

When she came back to earth, Eli kissed her, then lowered her to the floor of the tub, making sure she caught her balance before leading her to the spray of the shower.

Then he proceeded to wash her hair for her, massaging her scalp with his large, blunt fingers. He washed her, causing her heart to melt even more.He turned off the shower and grabbed a towel from the stack waiting by the shower. He wrapped it around her, then kissed the tip of her nose.

"I'm going to marry you, you know," he said. "As soon as I can."

She gasped and stepped out of the circle of his arms.

Her blood was roaring in her ears. She could see Eli talking, but couldn't hear anything he said over the constant litany of *No, no, no!* in her thoughts.

She stumbled into the bedroom, Eli hot on her heels. Her towel dropped, and she stepped into a pair of yoga pants and pulled a faded t-shirt over her head.

"I'm going to go get a snack," she blurted, cutting off whatever Eli had been saying.

His eyes narrowed, and he reached for her only to drop his arms back to his sides. She could see the curse he said. He nodded.

And then she just fled.

"No, no, no," she now said aloud as she made her frantic way to the kitchen.

Marry her?

He didn't even love *her.*

If she married him, it would be bad. Horrible.

She would be trapped with someone who expected her to be perfect. Again.

A lifetime of stepping on eggshells? Of constantly disappointing the man she loved? Of slowly driving him away as he realized she wasn't who he expected?

"No, no, no!"

She crashed into the kitchen, bumping into the doorframe on her way. It was dark. She couldn't see the patterned wallpaper or any of the furniture. She was alone, and therefore, able to take a deep breath.

She filled her lungs to capacity, then blew the air out through parted lips. It calmed her and allowed her to begin breathing again. With the increased oxygen came a certain degree of clarity.

Yikes. She may have bungled that.

Like, really hard.

She remembered how badly she'd reacted to Eli's first awkward confession of love and winced. She owed him an apology.

And maybe an explanation, psycho? the Voice piped in.

Abilene rolled her eyes. Yeah, she owed him that, too.

Hope flared. If she explained the perfect-thing to Eli, maybe he would understand. Maybe he could love her for her . . . .

She grabbed the Oreos from the table and spun around to jog back up to the bedroom.

But a silhouette stood in the doorway.

"Eli?" Abilene asked.

She knew it wasn't Eli. The silhouette was curvy. Voluptuous. Female.

The silhouette moved forward until she was standing in a beam of moonlight. The silver light reflected off of her dark brown hair and mocha skin.

"Dahlia?" Abilene almost couldn't believe what she was seeing. Dahlia's presence in Sergeant Collin's kitchen didn't compute. "What are you doing here?"

Dahlia looked different. It took Abilene a moment to discover it was Dahlia's eyes; they were cold. Flat.

Dangerous.

And suddenly, Abilene knew her earlier gut feeling was right. She was never going to see her friend again.

Because this woman in front of her was anything but her friend.

Chapter Seventeen

"You did always like the Oreos," Dahlia said. She took measured steps toward Abilene.

Abilene dropped the Oreos onto the counter. For every step Dahlia took toward her, she took one back.

"Dahlia, w-what's going on?" Abilene asked.

Dahlia's perfect teeth flashed in the moonlight, but the effect wasn't friendly. The woman's smile was all menace. "It's nice to see you up and about. We half expected you to be in your death-throes."

Abilene shook her head at words she didn't understand.

"I'm going to need you to come with me," Dahlia said, stalking ever closer.

The simple statement caused some of Abilene's fear to disappear. Anger replaced it. Abilene snorted. "Yeah, that's not going to happen. You want to tell me how long you've been working for the other side? How long you've been pretending to be my friend?" Abilene was damn pissed. She'd *liked* Dahlia. Had looked up to her.

Abilene felt the countertop at her back. As Dahlia kept advancing, the fear returned a thousand-fold. Abilene had no place to go. She was trapped.

Dahlia stopped in front of Abilene. "You *will* be coming with me," she said. "It'll be easiest if you comply."

Like hell. Abilene's fingers curled into a fist, and before she lost her courage, she struck out at Dahlia, aiming for the woman's face.

Her fist glanced off of Dahlia's cheek. Her head didn't even move. Abilene's heart sank.

Dahlia laughed softly. "He didn't teach you how to fight? Talk about negligence." She heard Dahlia crack her knuckles. "It's like this, little girl."

Dahlia's fist whipped toward Abilene's face.

Pain exploded like shrapnel in her left eye. Her head snapped back. Before Abilene could cry out, Dahlia's hand was crushing her mouth.

"You make one noise," the scent of cinnamon wafted over Abilene as the woman breathed her threat into Abilene's face, "and I'll kill the old man."

Holy God, who *was* this woman? Abilene nodded, and gasped in air as Dahlia released her.

"Why are you doing this?" Abilene couldn't prevent herself from asking as she felt around her eye. Nothing broken. Jeez, who knew a hit to the eye could hurt so much?

"That's a little clichéd, don't you think?" Dahlia tapped her bottom lip with one finger as she pondered Abilene. "I guess 'For reasons you wouldn't understand' is my line. If only I had a mustache to twirl. Now, if you don't mind. I'm in a hurry, and I don't trust you to keep your mouth shut." Before the words had even penetrated Abilene's brain, Dahlia was reaching toward Abilene's neck.

She felt a slight pinch, and then her world faded to black.

***

Eli gazed at the alarm clock as he paced around the bedroom.

Ten minutes. Abilene had been "getting a snack" for ten minutes.

God in heaven, what had ever possessed him to blurt out the marriage-thing like *that*? Was he *ever* going to be smooth around Abilene, or was he destined to be a bumbling cave man for the rest of their lives together?

Five more minutes. He would give her five more minutes, and then he would crawl down to the kitchen on his knees and beg her forgiveness.

And then he would do the marriage-thing right. Hell, maybe he'd even *ask* her this time instead of telling her.

Unease roiled through his stomach, but it had been doing so for the last five minutes. Eli tried his best to ignore it.

When three more minutes passed he thought, *Close 'nough.* The Voice piped in its agreement, and Eli was out the door moving as close to normal as he could manage in his urgency to reach Abilene.

He was surprised to find the kitchen light off, but it didn't slow him down. He felt the wall for the switch as he said, "Abilene, baby, I—"

The light clicked on. The kitchen was empty.

"Abilene?" he called softly, not yet willing to rouse the Sergeant if this proved to be nothing.

No answer.

Eli's pulse kicked into action. He made his way through the other rooms of the house, calling her name as he went. His voice was getting louder, but he didn't care.

He threw open the front door of the house and checked outside. The truck was still there. Abilene was nowhere in sight.

He rushed back into the house, ready to pound down Sergeant Collins' bedroom door, when he spotted the telephone in the hall.

The thing practically had a bull's eye painted on it. Eli walked toward it. He pressed the arrow on the caller id screen to see the last number dialed was a 760 area code. The tiny, pixilated screen read *Needles, CA.*

With an arm of lead, Eli picked up the receiver and hit redial. He pressed the phone to his ear and listened like a condemned man as an electronic voice announced, "Thank you for calling Needles Military Hospital. If this is an emergency, hang up and dial 911—"

Eli slammed the phone down.

His mouth went dry.

She'd done it.

Just as he'd always feared she would.

Abilene had betrayed him.

And his mom had been right; it fucking hurt.

"Son?" Sergeant Collins' voice came from behind Eli. Eli straightened and beat back the anguish he knew was painting his features before turning around to face Collins.

"Abilene called Major Taylor," Eli said in a dead voice. "And now she's gone. We have to move. It's not safe here anymore."

"You damn Johnsons," Sergeant Collins growled.

Eli snapped to attention in surprise. *Not* the reaction he was expecting.

"You and your mama—you're both the same. Always so ready to believe the worst about the people who love you." He walked forward and poked Eli in the shoulder. "How do you know Abilene called Major Taylor?"

Ow, damn. He rubbed his shoulder. "She made a call to the hospital in Needles, California?" Great. He'd said it like a question.

"Oh, well. That proves it. Let's just string the poor girl up right now," Collins groused as he pushed Eli back and grabbed the phone. The older man continued to grumble incoherent things as he jabbed in a phone number.

"Sergeant Collins here," he barked into the phone a second later. "A phone call was made from here about a half hour ago. I need to you trace it." There was a pause on Collins' side as the person on the phone said something. Something the Sergeant didn't like. "Don't make me repeat myself boy. Tell your superior officer this is Sergeant Collins calling."

Eli watched in wonder as the look on Collins' face revealed he was getting his way. Just who had this man become that his name got that sort of a reaction?

"Right," he pinned Eli with a glare, and Eli stepped back a pace. He couldn't help feeling like a kid in the principal's office. "And what towers did it ping off of?" Collins listened. "Any hotels, warehouses, or the like in that area where a hostage could be kept?"

Eli's mouth dropped. *What the hell?* Abilene a hostage?

He felt like a horrible man, but he wished with all of his might that it were true.

"Thanks. I'll put in a good word for you tomorrow, kid." And then Collins returned the phone to its cradle.

He crossed his arms over his barrel of a chest and tossed Eli a superior look. "That call your lady made was forwarded to a cell phone that pinged off of a tower here in Atlanta. There's a Hampton Inn by the tower that has outdoor room access." Collins shook his head. "She didn't betray you, son. She needs rescuing."

Eli frowned. So the call had gone to a cell phone here in Atlanta? "I'm sorry, Sarge. That sounds *worse*."

Sergeant Collins got into his face. "You stop this right now, boy. I met Abilene for a *second*, and it was enough for me to know she's head-over-heels for you. You keep this line of thinking up, and you *will* lose her. And you'll have no one to blame but yourself."

The Sergeant walked away from Eli to open a closet at the end of the hall. An entire arsenal of everything black and shiny was revealed to Eli, and he couldn't prevent a low whistle of appreciation.

"Now, are you going to help me go get her?" Collins asked. "Or are you going to sit here mooning over something that didn't happen like some kind of soft-bellied Yankee?"

Eli snarled. Sergeant Collins was poking at something that he didn't understand. Eli was right about Abilene, damn it. He just knew it!

But what if he's right? the Voice asked.

"Fine," Eli snapped, striding up to the closet and pulling several weapons from the racks. "But when we get there and find out she's with *them*, you're going to help me make her sorry."

Collins shook his head. "Just like your mama," he murmured as he filled his pockets with ammo.

Chapter Eighteen

Someone was prying Abilene's lips apart.

It was the first thing she'd known with absolute certainty since Sergeant Collin's kitchen.

She didn't know who that someone was, or why they were trying to pry her lips apart, but she knew two things: they were the enemy, and it couldn't be for her own good.

She tried her best to struggle, but she found that she was bound to whatever she was lying on.

Her eyes popped open in panic.

Looming over her were Major Taylor and Dahlia.

Dahlia was the one trying to open her mouth, and Major Taylor held something in one hand. The other arm was strapped to his chest.

Abilene's eyes flew to what was held in Taylor's hand.

Her gaze was riveted to what she saw.

He held a piece of fruit that resembled a slice of a peach. But only loosely.

The fruit looked like liquid gold. The part of the slice that would have held the pit was a deep bronze, and the skin of the fruit looked like glittering diamonds.

It was the most beautiful thing Abilene had ever seen.

Instinctively, she knew what it was.

This was *the* fruit.

Though her mouth watered for a taste—*demanded* a taste—she knew it would change her life forever.

It took all of her willpower, but Abilene continued to fight Dahlia to keep her mouth closed.

After several moments of struggle, Dahlia rolled her eyes and punched Abilene in the stomach.

Abilene would have cried out from the pain, but her diaphragm was paralyzed. And as soon as she opened her lips to attempt to gulp air, Major Taylor deposited the fruit into her mouth.

Juice from the fruit flowed over her tongue and down the back of her throat. *Sweet Jesus.* It tasted even better than it looked. It held the sharp tang of tropical fruit, but the smooth sweetness of melon.

It was heaven on earth.

She didn't have to be coerced into swallowing it. She gulped it down, and then looked for more as her mind screamed at her.

What have you done?

"Oh, God," she whimpered.

What now?

Major Taylor sighed and sank down on the bed next to her bound ankles. Relief colored his face. His cheeks flushed with color; his eyes brightened.

"It's done then," he said on another sigh. "She'll live. The Operation can continue."

Abilene's unease multiplied at the satisfaction on Taylor's face. If her eating the fruit had pleased him, she was in trouble.

She'll live? she repeated in her mind. *Half expected you to be in your death-throes. . . .* She looked back and forth between Dahlia and Major Taylor.

Major Taylor noticed her confusion, and his eyes softened. "I did always like you, Abilene. I'm sorry it had to be you." Abilene frowned.

"That he saw you first," Major Taylor clarified. "It could have been any of the girls, really, but it was you who stumbled upon him during the escape. An unfortunate turn of events."

Abilene was shaking her head. He'd only raised more questions with his cryptic explanation.

Taylor's shoulders slumped. "I suppose full disclosure is in order, hmm?" He turned to Dahlia. "Keep watch will you, my dear? Sergeant Collins is a man of many talents. I wouldn't be surprised if he were on his way here now."

Abilene held her breath. *Eli could be on his way?* God, she could only hope.

The moment the door closed, Abilene could feel change in the very air of the room. The atmosphere crackled.

Suddenly, Abilene's back bowed off of the bed in a wave of ecstasy.

Pleasure so intense it was on par with sex with Eli poured through her. Abilene's eyes closed, and she moaned aloud.

"And so it begins," Major Taylor said with disappointment.

Abilene was incapable of thought, but even she was able to recognize that this was the result of her indulgence in the fruit.

It was too wonderful to mourn.

Abilene moaned again as another wave hit her. She could feel it working through her, starting with the top of her head. When the gale left her, her vision was perfect. Better than she could ever remember it being.

She could see every pore on Major Taylor's face. The texture of the paint on the wall. Every edge was sharp. Every drab color in the dreary hotel room was vivid.

Abilene caught her reflection in the mirror above the dresser, and it took her a moment to recognize herself. Her appearance was changing before her eyes. Her features were realigning into perfection. She watched as the bump of her nose that she'd always hated disappeared.

"What's happening?" she gasped as she was bombarded yet again.

"Don't fret, it will be over soon," Taylor said instead of answering. "The other subjects' transformations took approximately five minutes."

For several more minutes, cresting sensation ruled Abilene's world. She noticed out of the corner of her eye that Major Taylor was observing her through a haze of arousal and sorrow. Her mind was too embroiled in her transformation to riddle the meaning of such disparate emotions.

Finally, Abilene could tell the sensations were lessening in intensity. She was able to take stock of her body.

And her vision wasn't the only thing that had changed. Her hearing was better. As was her sense of touch and smell. The flow of logic and reasoning came easily.

It was as though every human part of Abilene had been enhanced.

She lay shivering in the aftermath of the change. She began to ponder Major Taylor's confusing reaction during the past few minutes.

She knew she had crossed over into the realm of "them" in his mind. Though Major Taylor was the last person she wanted approval from, she still felt the sting of rejection. She couldn't help it.

"So, you've become Subject 4," he said, rising from the bed to put distance between them. "Pity."

Pity isn't all he's feeling, the Voice cautioned her.

With a start, Abilene realized even her connection to the Voice was also enhanced. Whereas before, it sounded as if she were being spoken to through a long, bounding hallway, now the Voice whispered into her ear.

She found it somehow comforting. Heartening. Courage flowed through her veins. Just a few minutes ago, she'd been wishing Eli would come and rescue her. Now, she knew she could rescue herself.

"I think it's time you told me everything," she said to the criminal she had watched murder the man she loved. The wretch who had tortured Eli for years. The man who had forced the fruit upon her.

She would use what that fruit gave her against him.

At her current enhanced status, he didn't have a prayer against her.

She knew it was too early to ask to be released, but the Voice hummed its approval as it sensed her plan to lure Major Taylor into a sense of complacency. Men had always underestimated her. She was, after all, just a helpless, delicate woman.

"Please, help me understand." Abilene turned her tone to pleading.

Major Taylor's mouth was held in a firm line of disapproval. His eyes glowered. "I'll assume Subject 3 has told you everything he knows, so I'll only divulge the information I know will be new to you," he began.

Abilene gritted her teeth against the heartless reference to Eli as a "subject." *Steady, girl,* she coached herself.

"What we never revealed to the participating subjects was the drastic reaction members of the opposite sex seemed to have to one another," Taylor continued. "Granted, we've only observed it in one—now two—couples. But you have all behaved consistently."

Major Taylor flicked his eyes toward the ceiling, his next words obviously unsavory to him. "There is an intense, chemical reaction between men and women when at least one of them has been introduced to the specimen. One of the more *religious* scientists compared it to the reaction Adam had to Eve in Genesis when he saw her for the first time."

Here, Major Taylor quoted from memory, "'This is now bone of my bones, and flesh of my flesh.' Once the subjects see each other, they recognize each other as mates, and an overwhelming sense of ownership pervades them.

"It's quite tedious, really," Taylor continued. "We named the process the Impulse. Once Subject 1 and 2 had skin-to-skin contact, they couldn't resist each other. They engaged in sexual intercourse," he spat the words, "within forty-eight hours."

Abilene couldn't prevent her blush. What Major Taylor was saying was a pretty apt description of what had happened between Eli and her.

Major Taylor noticed and nodded. "Then I'm correct in assuming that you experienced similar results?" He asked her as doctor-to-doctor, professional courtesy making a brief appearance in his voice.

Like it mattered. She wasn't answering such a damned personal question.

He took her silence for acquiescence. "Then I was right to move so quickly." Taylor noticed the question in her eyes. "Oh yes, there is good reason behind my actions, doctor. Subject 2, the female, died only three days after having intercourse with Subject 1."

Fear clutched Abilene in the chest.

"Carrying the offspring of an immortal turned out to be a fatal venture for the unaltered human," Taylor finished darkly.

For a moment, Abilene thought she might faint*Offspring*.

She'd had unprotected sex with Eli.

How had that happened? How had the possibility of pregnancy not even blipped on their radars? If she were her own patient, she'd kick her ass! But, oddly, Abilene didn't feel worry or anger.

She felt *joy*.

Eli's baby.

For the first time since discovering she was bound to the bed, Abilene struggled against the restraints. She wanted to cover her womb with her arms, to hug the child that might now be developing inside of her.

Please, God, let it be true, she whispered inside her skull.

Major Taylor sneered at her reaction. "Damn it, Abilene, you held such promise!" he exploded in an uncharacteristic display of anger. "And I even liked—" He stopped and shoved his good hand through his hair.

Liked you, the Voice whispered. *He liked you. Probably still does.*

And there Abilene had it: her way out.

It would take the best acting skills of her life, but it just might work.

Abilene didn't have to force her voice to tremble. "Major Taylor, this is . . ." *appalling*, "incredible! Do you realize what you've done?"

She had his attention again. He was looking at her with brows drawn and mouth slightly agape.

"You've single-handedly ensured that this country will never lose another war."

The slightest flicker of pride lit Major Taylor's eyes, but then he frowned, doubting her sincerity.

"That's precisely what I've done, doctor," he began. "And if you truly recognize the importance of these findings, you won't hesitate to cooperate in the Operation."

He was calling her bluff. And it was a brilliant move, because her body tried to physically reject Major Taylor's words. Abilene stifled the glower she felt molding her features, clamped down on the shiver of revulsion she felt at the suggestion.

She knew what he meant. Her *cooperation* meant nothing other than her being a brood mare. She would bear Eli's children, then immediately give up her parental rights: turn them over to this monster to extort.

Over my dead body.

She allowed herself a small smile over the irony of those words. Major Taylor saw it and narrowed his gaze.

She allowed her smile to widen and turn scolding. "Major Taylor, it appears as though my 'cooperation' is a done-deal, whether I wish it or not."

Yes, the Voice whispered. *He knows you would not capitulate easily. Make him work for it.*

He nodded. "I will not pretend it is otherwise; however, your willingness, or lack thereof, can have an impact on many things." He cocked an eyebrow. His question was clear: *So what will it be?*

She nodded as well and assumed an expression of contemplation. He watched her. While the silence grew oppressive, Abilene's mind scurried for facets of Taylor's personality to use against him.

He was neat. Orderly. Abhorred mess of any kind, and above all, viewed any sign of humanity as a weakness.

The Impulse, the Voice guided. *He spoke of the Impulse with disgust.*

Perfect.

Um . . .thanks, she mentally whispered back. This new dialogue between them was going to take some getting used to.

She drew in a deep breath and held it until her lungs burned. It was a physical sign that she had come to a decision, and Major Taylor recognized it as such. He straightened where he stood; his eyes grew wary.

He fully expected her to tell him to go fuck himself. It was written across his face.

And his instincts were dead-on, because that is precisely what she wanted to say to him.

Instead, Abilene said, "I won't lie, Taylor. I don't appreciate coercion. Did you think to simply tell me the truth and *ask* me if I would participate? Did you think I would turn an opportunity like this down?" She scoffed. "This is the type of research to make or break a professional, and I'm looking to make a name for myself. I would have been in the bag."

Taylor's eyes widened, but otherwise he gave no reaction to her words.

More, said the Voice.

"And now you've exposed me to this . . .*Impulse.* Do you have any idea what that's like for me? To be out of control of myself in such a . . .*disgusting* way." Abilene's voice grew impassioned. "It completely took my free will away. If I had been given the choice, I would have never chosen a man like Eli for myself. I would have chosen a man like y—"

She stopped mid-word, allowed her eyes to flutter down as though she were embarrassed, and hoped like hell she was managing to blush.

In her peripheral vision, she saw Major Taylor take a stumbling step forward, then stop himself.

Bull's eye, she and the Voice thought simultaneously.

She brought her eyes up to his face again, and was pleased to notice that Taylor's form wavered through a sheen of moisture. She deserved a freakin' Oscar.

"Please," she paused to swallow, "*please*, tell me there's a cure to this feeling. I'll help the Operation. I'll help you capture Eli." *Not a possibility.* "I'll do *anything*, Major, just . . .help me."

Taylor just looked at her. His face was stoic, but his eyes. . . . His eyes gave it all away.

They were bright and hopeful. If he had written her a script of the right things to say to him to convince him she was salvageable, it wouldn't have been more effective than the performance she'd just delivered.

Finally, Taylor moved. He shuffled to the bed, stalling several times before committing, and moved to awkwardly untie her wrists and ankles with one hand. She held her breath the entire time, sure that at any second, he would find her out as a liar.

When the strips of bed sheets that had functioned as her restraints were undone, Abilene sat up and rubbed her aching wrists. Major Taylor retreated to the chair by the door and scrubbed a hand down his face.

That's when Abilene noticed his pistol—the very same pistol he had used to shoot Eli. It lay on the end table between two armchairs; the warm light of the table lamp gleamed off of its metallic surface.

She looked away, lest Taylor see it and glean her thoughts.

She needed that gun. If she could get her hands on it, she could. . . .

What? Kill him?

God, could she?

The revulsion she'd felt at Taylor's suggestion of cooperation returned a hundred-fold with the idea of taking a life. Even a life as abhorrent as that of Major Taylor.

She swallowed the bile that had risen in her throat. No, she couldn't kill him.

And your other option is what? the Voice asked.

Major Taylor spoke, jolting her from her crowded thoughts. "You must forgive my skepticism, Abilene, but given the circumstances, I'm afraid you're going to have to prove where your loyalty lies."

She frowned at him.

"You spoke of helping us capture Eli. . . ."

***

Eli watched as Sergeant Collins subdued the kicking Hispanic woman they'd seen leaving the hotel room they suspected was working as Taylor's base. She was fighting the man like a hellcat. It was actually pretty impressive.

Eli stood ready to step in if the woman got in another left hook, but he wasn't ready to make such a move, yet. He knew Sergeant Collins wouldn't appreciate needing an assist.

Collins cursed as the woman bit the hand covering her mouth, but he didn't remove his fingers. The woman attempted to scream something that sounded like *cabrón* into Collins's hand.

After several more seconds of struggle, Collins managed to put the woman out with a well-placed pinch. Both men sighed in relief as she slumped to Collins's feet.

Damn, she'd almost been a more formidable foe than Taylor.

Collins's breath was bellowing in and out of his body as he leaned over and braced his hands on his knees. "Well, I think we found out where they are," he said between gulps of air. "There's no way a civilian would have fought like that."

Eli studied the woman's prone form. *Enlisted?*

He shook his head. There was time later to iron out all the particulars.

"I'll maintain the perimeter," Collins stated. "You go on ahead and get our girl, Eli. And be rehearsing ways you can beg her forgiveness for doubting her."

It was perhaps the millionth time Collins had made a comment like that since they'd left the house. And, just like all the other times, hope flared in Eli's chest, but it was squelched by doubt.

Finding a woman in Taylor's employ solidified the possibility that Abilene was working with the man.

Eli nodded once, then crept toward the hotel room door that was his mark. He kept to the shadows as much as he could with the bright moonlight illuminating the crumbling parking lot of the hotel.

When he reached the door, he pressed his back to the wall beside the frame, the Sig Sauer in his left hand resting against his thigh.

With no increased effort on Eli's part, the words of Abilene filled Eli's ears: *Please.... I'll help you capture Eli.*

Eli's world turned on its head.

He didn't realize he'd held onto a large portion of hope where Abilene's loyalty was concerned until he heard her offer to help capture him. The devastation he felt upon hearing those words taught him he had new depths of despair to discover in his life.

He'd thought he'd hit rock bottom in the lab.

He hadn't even been close.

Abilene would do anything to capture Eli for Major Taylor, to help the experiments—including pretending to be a victim.

And Eli had fallen for it, too. Hook, line, and sucker.

The weight of his body was almost too much for his bones. He wanted to sink down to the chilled sidewalk and hold his head in his hands.

But he couldn't do that with a gun in his hand.

So, I go to Plan B, he thought. *I can wallow after.*

Rage swept in. He felt the Voice's disapproval, but the Voice had been oddly quiet since Eli had heard Abilene's treachery.

Eli took that as an indication that he was right.

He swung around, and with a quick, violent turn of the doorknob, broke the flimsy lock. He opened the door and laid eyes on the woman he had proposed to tonight.

Abilene looked small sitting in the middle of the queen-sized bed. Her wrists were red and raw, and even through his hate, Eli felt a twinge of anger that she was hurt, even in this slight way.

And then he noticed that her wrists were healing. Really quickly. His eyes snapped back up to her face. It was perfect.

Eli lost it.

"You fucking son of a bitch," he wheeled on Taylor and had his hand around the man's throat before Taylor had even seen him move. "You *turned* her?" Eli's grip tightened, and Taylor's face grew read; his eyes bulged.

They planned this! Before he could exact his revenge on the tormentor, Eli had to address Abilene.

He released Taylor, not even paying notice to how the man collapsed to his knees, coughing and gasping. He turned around and pinned Abilene with the most hateful glare he could muster.

She huddled in on herself further. "E-Eli—" she began. He stalked closer, cutting her words off with a feral growl.

"I don't want to hear your lies. You betrayed me," he spat. "I don't let that go unpunished."

Yet, even as Abilene's eyes grew wide with fear, he knew he couldn't hurt her. The Voice raised its proverbial hackles at the idea.

No, it would be going against Eli's own body to hurt this woman, and the realization fueled his anger and hurt. That she could so lightly set him aside when it appeared that he would be under her spell for all of his immortal existence. . . .

Abilene's eyes darted to the left to look at a spot over Eli's shoulder, and Eli spun around just as Major Taylor launched himself at Eli.

Eli took the man's full weight to his chest, and his air whooshed out of him. His stomach seized.

Both men hit the floor with a cacophonous clash of bones and flesh. Abilene faded from Eli's mind as he focused on the man who had ruined everything.

Eli felt something akin to euphoria as he realized he was going to finally—*finally*—get revenge on the man who had tortured him for nearly a decade. The man who had stolen his soul. The man who had facilitated his heart-break.

Eli felt a surge of power and anger. He tossed Taylor off him. He scrambled on top of the man, pinning Taylor's shoulders with his knees. Eli prepared to pummel the man's face to pulp, but a quick, black blur to the left of his face announced that Taylor had gotten his hands on Eli's Sig.

Light exploded in Eli's left eye as the butt of his own pistol crushed his eye socket. Eli sagged for a second as he absorbed the pain, but it was all Taylor needed to gain the upper hand.

Eli was on his back looking up at Taylor as the Tormentor leveled the business end of the Sig Sauer between Eli's eyes.

It was going to be another kill shot.

Eli had failed. Again.

He would wake up in the laboratory. Again.

And Abilene had ensured it would happen.

Major Taylor's cheeks were pink with exertion and pure animal pleasure. His breath was billowing in and out of his chest as though he were with a lover. It was so similar to all of the other times Eli's death had come at the hands of this monster that all of the fight drained out of Eli.

Eli would never win against this man. He hadn't in the past, and he never would. The Tormentor bettered Eli at every turn.

Eli didn't have the strength to fight anymore. His mother was dead, the woman he loved had betrayed him, and he was about to kiss Death once more.

What was there left to fight for?

Eli sighed, the motion causing Major Taylor to rise and fall. Then Eli closed his eyes and waited. Waited for the report of the pistol. The smell of the burning powder. The explosion of bone and blood.

The peace of the end.

For the first time in eight years, Eli craved the silence, the calm, that followed death. He was just so damned tired.

The pistol exploded in a jolt so powerful, Eli felt Major Taylor's body buck. Eli braced himself for the pain.

After a few seconds, Eli's brows drew together. It didn't hurt this time. Had he gotten so used to gruesome deaths that he was numb to the pain?

What a blessing that would be in the coming months.

He opened his eyes slowly, not willing to jostle his body and bring on the agony.

The first thing he saw was half of Major Taylor's face. He blinked again, hoping to dispel the foggy confusion. When he looked again, Eli discovered his eyes had not deceived him.

Half of Major Taylor's head was gone. A jagged crescent was carved out of the left side of Taylor's head.

Eli's eyes flew to the shaking form of Abilene where she stood behind Taylor's lifeless but still erect form. Abilene held a gun that Eli recognized as Major Taylor's in her right hand, and it still pressed against Major Taylor's right temple.

And for the rest of his immortal life, Eli would never forget the look on her face. He expected to see hysterical female. What he saw instead was pure warrior. Abilene's mouth was set in a grim, determined line. Her eyes were cold, unfeeling, as she observed Taylor's body. Except for the slight shaking of her body, she was a rock.

Gravity claimed the body's equilibrium. Taylor's body slid to the left, off of Eli's chest, and onto the floor. Eli's face turned to look at his Tormentor, and they were nose to nose until Eli scrambled away.

When his back smacked against the wall, halting his progress, he looked at Abilene again. "You *killed* him."

She shrugged. "He was going to hurt you."

The man, who Eli had fantasized about killing for years but had never been able to defeat, lay dead a few feet away. In the end, Eli hadn't gotten his own revenge. He hadn't saved the girl.

She had saved him.

As Abilene laid the tormentor's pistol on the bed, Eli felt a swelling of love for this amazing woman. He could feel it alter the planes of his face and knew that he was looking at her as if she were his life, but he couldn't temper his reaction.

He waited for her expression to mirror his, as it had many times over the last few days when they had a moment together, when their feelings for one another had overwhelmed them both.

But Abilene remained resolute. Her eyes never lost their arctic chill. Her face never lost its determined aura.

She turned toward the door, and Eli watched in disbelief as she took measured, deliberate steps across the hotel room.

In shock Eli realized she was leaving.

Leaving him.

"*Abilene*," he implored, his voice breaking.

She stopped but didn't turn around.

"Where—" *are you going?* Eli couldn't bring himself to finish the sentence, terrified of the answer.

"Did you think I would miss the part where you thought I was working with *him*?" she whispered.

Devastating shame became the center of Eli's world. He remembered with vivid clarity the way he had stormed into the room. The accusation in his voice. The plans he had to hurt and destroy, not just Major Taylor, but Abilene as well, knowing that she'd betrayed him just as he'd always suspected she would.

He'd been so sure.

He'd been such a fucking idiot.

"I was wrong, Abilene," he stammered. "So wrong—"

She cut him off. "Save it. You don't *see* me, Eli. You'll always be wrong. 'You're perfect. You're a liar. You betrayed me.' The point is, I'm *me*. And you're not willing to find out who that is if it doesn't fit *your* definition of 'Abilene.'"

Eli's head snapped back at the power of her words.

"Goodbye, Eli." Abilene's voice held not one iota of hesitation as her hand moved to the doorknob and turned.

Eli made a noise of distress, but Abilene didn't slow down as she walked off into the night leaving the door open behind her.

The air he needed to speak nearly drowned him as his chest spasmed in horror. "Abilene!" he bellowed at the top of his lungs. In the space of a heartbeat, Eli was on his feet and pounding pavement to get to her.

But she'd had enough of a head start to get to the truck. Eli watched as his traitor of a mentor handed Abilene the keys, then held the door open for her as she climbed in.

She threw the truck into reverse amidst a violent grinding of gears, and Eli put on a greater burst of speed as she switched into first gear and began to drive off with haste.

He knew he was screaming her name, but he couldn't hear it over the roar of blood in his ears.

He'd ruined *everything*. She was leaving.

Pulling out of the parking lot.

Gone.

Eli continued to run after the truck long after its taillights had faded into oblivion.

Seconds passed into minutes. Minutes collected.

Eli turned around and began the torturous walk back to the hotel parking lot. Sergeant Collins was standing just where Eli had left him: over the trussed-up form of the woman they'd subdued before Eli had destroyed everything good in his life.

The older man gazed at Eli with a mixture of sympathy and grim anger, and Eli knew that Collins sensed everything that had transpired, from Eli's betrayal of his woman to Abilene's actions. Eli wanted to be mad himself, at Collins, but he couldn't get over the feeling of loss that was crippling him. He stared at Collins for a bit. Finally, "You helped her leave me."

"You're damn right I did," he said in a low voice.

Collins words rolled over Eli, and Eli nodded in acknowledgement. *Message received.*

Eli knew he had been wrong. Couldn't be more sorry. Knew beyond absolute certainty that he would never doubt Abilene again.

It no longer mattered.

"Do you know where she's gone?" Eli asked.

Collins nodded but said only, "She's safe." The *from the likes of you* was implied. "You have five minutes to pull yourself together, son," Collins said gently now. "Then the Army will be here. We'll both be taken into official custody as they clean this mess up and figure out what happened to you for all of these years. You'll need your wits about you."

Eli's world had stopped on its axis with Abilene's departure. That he would now be expected to continue on, to explain the past eight years, to account for all of the horrors he had encountered . . . .

Eli dropped to his knees. The gravel from the parking lot tore into his jeans, but he paid it no mind. He groaned in intense emotional pain, a sentiment the Voice echoed.

"I'm sorry," he whispered, hoping the apology found its way across the miles.

Eli heard the crunch of gravel beneath official tires. He straightened and resigned himself to what was about to come.

***

Though tears streamed down her face, Abilene had no trouble discerning the road through the truck's windshield. In the back of her mind, the tiny part that wasn't screaming at her in anguish for leaving Eli, Abilene recognized that she should at least be seeing a blur. Her vision was flawless.

Another reminder of how everything had changed.

You did the right thing, the Voice assured her.

Abilene sniffed in abject misery. She *knew* that.

It didn't make this easier.

She already missed Eli with a physical ache.

The point is, I'm me, she'd said to him. The problem was, she didn't really know what that meant, either. Everything she'd accused Eli of—she was just as guilty.

Well, maybe it was time to change that. Once and for all.

Another wave of emotional pain wafted over her, and she bent forward over the steering wheel and sobbed anew.

Abilene, honey, use your brain. Distract yourself, the Voice whispered.

She sat up straight and wiped her runny nose with one forearm. Right. Distract herself.

It was something she'd done many times as a kid to escape the hell of growing up under a microscope. She'd always gone over what she'd learned in science class that day—her favorite subject.

So, what had she learned in science today?

She snorted. *That immortality is real?* She caught the reflection of her freakishly pretty eyes in the rearview mirror.

She was going to live forever.

It hit her for the first time. How was that even possible? What had been done to her body that would allow her to live forever?

The human body had a very finite existence. The Hayflick limit—the number of times a cell could divide before dying—ensured that everyone had an expiration date.

But there were scientists who had lengthened the Hayflick limit in lab mice. . . . Abilene wracked her brain. What chemical had they used?

Something niggled in Abilene's brain.

And like a tumbler, everything clicked into place.

With one hand, Abilene wrenched open the glove compartment and pulled out any and every piece of loose paper she could find. She grabbed a pen off of the floorboard and kept one eye on the road as she steered with one hand and wrote with the other.

Ideas flowed from Abilene's brain to the paper at an inhuman rate.

It may have been minutes, hours, or days, but the next time Abilene really looked at her surroundings, she realized she was sitting in the Duke parking lot.

Right in front of the lab building.

She flicked a glance at the dashboard clock and saw that it was right before dawn. Abilene drummed her fingers on the dashboard.

Duke *did* have an all-night laboratory.

Abilene gathered all the crumpled, coffee-stained paper she had written on, wrenched open the door, and headed toward the front door of the building as quickly as she could.

Chapter Nineteen

Abilene gave the two young recruits who were standing in front of her desk the snake eye until their gazes wavered and fell to their shoes. Since replying to her military summons, she'd known this day was bound to come.

After all, telling the United States Army to go fuck themselves, in writing no less, rarely yielded positive results.

Abilene's gaze wandered around her office, and she allowed herself a rare moment of indulgent pride as she considered all she had accomplished in the past couple of months. Her eyes were drawn to the frames dotting her wall. It wasn't Abilene's decorating style of choice, but her assistant had framed several of the articles that had been written about Abilene's research. They were posted on the wall among an impressive handful of awards. On Abilene's desk lay the letter from the Norwegian Nobel Committee that she had received today.

She had been nominated for the Nobel Prize.

She, Abilene Miller, screw-up of the modern world, had finally come into her own. She still had trouble believing it.

The night she'd ended up at Duke had marked a new beginning. She'd spent a few more nights in the lab before she'd visited an old professor to show him what she'd been working on. Pure shock and awe had lit his face when she'd explained her theory on the Hayflick limit and the implication on human immortality.

The next three months had been a flurry of grant applications, late-night labs, and unwanted publicity as her research became famous.

And hanging over it all was Eli.

She missed him with a constant ache that often became actual physical pain. She'd realized what she had to do to stem the debilitating lust that struck like clock-work every few hours, but the orgasms she brought herself were hollow, and infuriatingly, only made her miss and love Eli even more.

She had hoped distance would cure her feelings. Instead, distance had enriched them. And she didn't have too long to figure out what she was going to do about the other quickly-growing wrinkle in her plan to forget Eli.

She rested a hand over the slight bulge beneath her rib cage as she brought herself out of the prison of her thoughts to nail the recruits with another glare.

"Would you mind repeating that again, gentlemen? I fear I've misheard you." Her tone dared them to repeat their missive.

The blond one on the right cleared his throat and, without looking up from his boots, said, "Your presence is requested in Washington. You leave in an hour."

Rather than dignify them with a response, Abilene continued to stare them down as she drummed her fingers against the glossy surface of her cherry-wood desk. Before long, she had both men squirming in their dress uniforms.

Ah, yes, she congratulated herself, silently. She had, indeed, become a badass.

"I'm sure you'll understand that it's quite impossible for me to leave my research at this time," she said. The words themselves were pleasant enough, but the young men were not fooled. If they continued to try to strong-arm Abilene to Washington, it would be at their own peril.

There was a knock at her open door, and Abilene swung her gaze to see her wide-eyed assistant. Abilene frowned. Her assistant was never wide-eyed.

"Excuse me, ma'am," she began, "but the president is on the phone."

Abilene stifled irritation. The president of Duke was always calling her. "Please tell him I'll call back later," she said.

Her assistant remained in the door. Abilene's frown deepened.

"I'm sorry, doctor," her assistant continued. "It's the President. Of the United States."

The men standing in front of her desk exchanged relieved glances, and Abilene only *just* prevented herself from swearing.

It looked like she was going to Washington.

"I'll meet you out front, gentlemen," Abilene sighed as she reached for the phone.

***

Eight harrowing hours later, Abilene stood in front of a solid metal door between her two escorts, clutching her overnight bag to her chest. Both men had repeatedly offered to carry her bag for her, but she liked how it doubled as a shield.

She may have changed a lot in the past months, but she was still wary in new situations.

And she had no idea what she was doing here. Both men had been silent as the grave, each refusing to answer her questions.

A security camera panned over them, and then she heard the click of the door unlocking. It opened toward them, and Abilene's mouth dropped open.

She knew *exactly* why she was here.

The door had opened to reveal a vast, domed room. It looked like the inside of the botanical gardens she'd visited as a kid. The building housing the room had appeared like it was solid brick, but from inside the room, Abilene could see that it was only camouflaged to appear so. The squared walls of the building were not fully opaque. Sunlight filtered through the illusion of brick and streamed through the glass dome that was nestled in the middle of the building like a ball in a box. Men and women wearing lab coats walked from one side of the room to another, entering and exiting what appeared to be labs and offices.

Two magnificent, fully-grown trees stood in the very center of the room. Thick, virile roots sprang from their trunks and plowed into the dirt that made up the floor of the dome. The trees' leafy branches stretched out to brush against the glass walls.

Abilene recognized the fruit hanging from one of the trees as the specimen she'd been forced to eat. The other tree held fruit in the shape of a pomegranate that was swirled black and white. The colors of the fruit moved rather than remained still. The pattern the black and white made was mesmerizing.

Abilene sucked in a breath. *These are the Tree of Life and the Tree of the Knowledge of Good and Evil.*

And right on the heels of that thought: *Eli is here.*

Her traitorous heart leapt.

"If you'll excuse me, ma'am," the man to her left said as he gripped her elbow, "you have an appointment that begins," he paused to look at his watch, "five minutes ago."

Abilene nodded as he led her toward an office on the other side of the dome. She couldn't take her eyes off of the trees, and her escorts noticed. The blond chuckled. "Yeah, that's how we all react when we first see them." He shook his head. "It's *still* a struggle to not just stand there and stare all day."

Abilene could empathize as she twisted her head at an awkward angle to keep the trees in view. She didn't see the men stop, and so she plowed full tilt into one of them.

He grunted and stepped forward to catch himself. Abilene blushed. She peeked around his shoulder to see they were standing in front of an office. The door had a brass name plate that read *Sergeant Collins: Co-Director.*

Her heart leapt again, but this time Abilene didn't curse it. The man hadn't contacted her in the last three months, and she hadn't seen him but that once, but he was important to Abilene. They'd connected on a high level.

She was eager to see him.

"I'm meeting with Sergeant Collins?" she asked. Suddenly she was more than ready to get this show on the road.

Rather than answer her, the blond opened the door for her, and the men moved to flank each side of the door. Abilene eyeballed them again. They were young and handsome.

Quiet and cute. Why couldn't I like one of them? she thought as she moved through the door and closed it behind her. She was ruined for all other men.

And then she spotted Collins behind his desk. As soon as she had entered the room, the man stood. His eyes were glowing as he looked her over with concern. His face morphed into a smile, all of his wrinkles on display, and he moved around the desk to stand before her and catch both of her hands between his own.

"Abilene, dear, I'm so glad you could make it."

She couldn't prevent the smile that stole over her features at his warm greeting, but she did manage to pull her hands out of his and pin him with an accusatory stare. Well, as accusatory as she could manage in her joy.

"Sergeant, you know I was dragged here against my will."

"Earl, please." He gestured to one of the armchairs sitting in front of his desk, and while she settled herself, Sergeant Collins seated himself in the chair next to her rather than on the other side of the desk. He took her hands once more. "How have you been, dear?" he asked, his gaze probing.

She knew he wasn't talking about generalities. He was asking about Eli. Abilene blinked. Hard. It was enough to stem the tears she could feel stinging the backs of her eyes. "Busy," she said noncommittally.

That adoring grin split his face once more. "Yes, I know that." He gestured with a nod toward a bulging file folder on his desk. Abilene could see newspaper and magazine article clippings protruding from its depths. It touched her. Sergeant Collins had followed her recent success. So had her parents, as it turned out, and they had been calling lately, hoping to create a relationship with their daughter now that she wasn't an embarrassment. She'd been permanently unavailable.

But Sergeant Collins had liked her always, even when she was all untapped potential. It meant so much more that he had clipped all of her press. And from the looks of the dog-eared, stained folder, the contents had been visited often.

"I'm so proud of you, honey," Collins confirmed.

Damn it. Now the tears came, and she had no hope of stemming the flow. Damn her hormones. Sergeant Collins just looked at her and pulled an actual handkerchief out of his pocket as he patted her back.

God, Southern men are a breed apart, Abilene thought as she took the handkerchief and blotted at her tears. She had to admit, she'd missed the manners she'd gotten so used to in that short amount of time.

Once Abilene had herself under control again, she gave Collins a watery smile, and he took that as his cue to continue. "You're here, Abilene, because we want to hire you."

We? Abilene frowned. That better not mean who she thought it meant.

"The United States government," the Sergeant clarified.

But Abilene was already shaking her head. It didn't matter who was trying to hire her—Collins, the government, or Eli—she wasn't looking for a job doing . . .whatever it is they were doing that involved the trees. If she was going to maintain her distance from Eli, working with him was out.

"Now, just hold on there, girlie," Collins chided. "Why don't you let me explain the job and why we want you?" Abilene hesitated. "What could it hurt, huh?"

Abilene clenched her teeth. In the end, she knew she couldn't deny Collins anything. She would steel herself to the possibility. *Wait him out. As soon as he's done talking, just say no. Easy-peasy.*

But actually listen, the Voice whispered.

Collins launched into his explanation of the job, probably guessing that if he waited a moment longer, Abilene would refuse him.

Against her better judgment, Abilene was soon listening to the Sergeant's explanation avidly, even scooting to the edge of her chair in her excitement.

Damn it, but this was her golden goose. They wanted her to do genetic research for them: continue her current work, but with unlimited funding; complete run of her own laboratory; and as many young, intelligent recruits as she wanted to work for her.

She would have *carte blanche*. Butterflies fluttered in her stomach. She could accomplish so much. This would make all of the difference.

And from the smug look on Sergeant Collins' face, he knew he was offering her something she would be unable to refuse.

Bastard, she thought fondly. After all, how mad could she be at the man who was handing her her dreams? It was almost too good to be true.

For a second, old doubts crept in. *Why* would he offer her this position? She was still young, inexperienced. Sure, she'd proved herself, but....

Eli.

Collins wanted to hire her because of Eli. Not because she was some laboratory rock star, but because she was connected to Eli. Knew Secrets. Was a liability.

"Stop," she whispered. Collins halted so quickly, she may as well have yelled the word. "I have to know why."

Collins frowned. "I don't understand, honey. Why what?"

"Are you wanting to hire me so you can keep a close eye on me? Because of the. . . *relationship* I had with Eli?

Collins laughed. "Are you kidding me?" He chuckled again.

But she didn't hear him over a new thought had planted itself in her brain. She groaned. "Oh God, does everybody out there know?" Her escorts? All of those scientists? Did they think she was a slut? Eli's cast-offs?

You *left* him, *remember?* the Voice said. *If anything, he's* your *cast-offs*. She winced. Ironically, she didn't like the Voice talking about Eli that way.

Collins cleared his throat, which drew Abilene's attention back to his face. She drew back in shock. He looked *pissed*. "Now you listen here, young lady. I thought you were smarter than this. Thought you'd proved so when you left Eli in the dust for doubting you. And now you doubt yourself? Hell, maybe you're not smart enough for this position after all."

He clucked his tongue. "I want to hire you because you're a gol-dang genius with a microscope, as most of the country, and now the world knows, you crazy woman. And now we're getting ready to begin testing the other tree, and we're not willing to risk the integrity of the experiments on anyone less qualified than the current leading research specialist in immortality." He pinned her with a glare. "That's you, in case you forgot."

Abilene swallowed and resisted the urge to look at her feet like a kid in the principal's office. She heard Collins mutter something about being surrounded by "idjiots" and smiled.

He rose to his feet and headed toward the door. "Take some time to think about it while you tour the lab." When Collins opened the door, he snapped his fingers at the blond recruit who was still waiting outside of the door. "Private Stevens here will be your guide. Take her wherever she wants, son," he said to the soldier, and then he walked out while Abilene stared at his back.

He'd been right of course. Her confidence in herself still took some cultivating. She sighed and smiled at Private Stevens. "Ready whenever you are, I guess."

He nodded and headed out of the door. She followed on his heels.

Over the next hour, Abilene fell more and more in love with the state-of-the-art facility that Collins was co-directing. They had everything she could ever hope to want or anticipate needing. She was becoming more and more convinced that she was going to have to accept this job or admit she was indeed an "idjiot."

Then Stevens stopped in front of an observation room and led the way in. "These are our test subjects," the young recruit said. Abilene gazed through the one-way mirror, anxious to see under what conditions the subjects were kept. Anything inhumane would, of course, be a deal-breaker.

"You're not…killing anyone here, are you?" she asked curtly.

Stevens's eyes widened. His mouth flopped open.

Thank God. "Just checking," she said.

The one-way mirror looked out over two separate rooms that were set up much like college dorm rooms, but with a lot more luxury. In the room on Abilene's left, a mammoth man, even impossibly bigger than Eli, lay on his back on the extra-long twin bed. His forearm lay across his eyes. He exuded an aura of misery. Abilene's heart went out to him.

"The subjects, of course, are here under their own volition. The co-directors would have it no other way," Stevens said hastily at the look on Abilene's face. She relaxed.

"Then why does he look so. . . ." she drifted off.

Stevens nodded. "That's part of the reason he asked to stay on in the experiment. He's Subject 1. Jericho. He lost his mate many years ago and has lost the will to live. As you know, the immortal subjects have no option but to live. He figured he may as well help the Operation as a willing volunteer than try to face the outside world without her. His door is always unlocked, but he never leaves his room."

"Wow, that's. . . ." *horrible.* Poor man.

Her eyes drifted to the left and she viewed the other subject for the first time. Her heart stopped.

Dahlia.

Abilene stepped forward, her hands coming up to the mirror.

"What the fuck is she doing here?" Abilene snarled.

The young soldier stepped back. "Y-you know her?"

Oh yeah, she did. Abilene wished like hell that the mirror wasn't there. That she could get her hands around the other woman's delicate neck. She looked at the other soldier, confirming without a word that she did, indeed, know the woman on the other side of the glass.

"She's testing the other fruit. The co-directors didn't reveal much, but it's clear that she chose to work for the Operation to get out of jail time for something pretty bad. The rumor is she killed someone." He looked at Abilene hopefully, as though she would confirm or deny the gossip.

Dream on, kid.

Dahlia sat on her own bed, her elbows braced on her knees, her face devoid of emotion. The bed she was sitting on shared a wall with the bed in Jericho's room, and Abilene felt protective of the man who lay prone in his room by himself. She didn't like that Dahlia was so near to him.

That woman was pure misery herself.

Stevens cleared his throat. "Would you like to meet with the other director now?" he asked, obviously not sure if he'd done something that would sway Abilene's decision to join the Operation or not.

Abilene nodded. She was ready to get out of this room.

At least, she was until she saw the name on the other director's door.

Eli Johnson: Co-Director.

Abilene's mouth went dry in a mix of anticipation and trepidation.

"I'll just leave you here, ma'am," the recruit said as he beat a hasty retreat. She felt sorry for the kid. She'd not kept a handle on her emotions well. Again, her hand went to her abdomen.

Well, she'd have to face the man sooner or later. She did have news that he deserved to hear.

This is not going to be easy.

She twisted the knob and tried to leave her heart at the door. She didn't succeed.

Eli Johnson sat behind a mahogany desk. His dark head was bent over a pile of paperwork, and the pen in his right hand moved back and forth. He didn't look up when she entered, so she had a moment to view him uninterrupted.

Her eyes drank him in.

Her heart hurt. She'd known she'd missed him, had craved him, loved him. But she hadn't been prepared for the experience seeing him again after months of separation would be.

"I'll be with you in just a moment," Eli's spoke into his pile of paperwork in that deep voice that turned Abilene's legs to jelly.

She moaned before she could stop herself.

Eli's head flew up. His pupils dilated the moment his eyes found her huddled against the door, and his lids widened. His mouth parted.

"Abilene," he breathed.

He shot to his feet and took two steps toward her before catching himself and stopping. He leaned against the corner of his desk as though his legs couldn't quite hold himself.

They stared at each other way longer than was acceptable for future co-workers.

"Hi," Abilene squeaked to break the silence.

Eli's eyes closed at the sound of her voice, and just like that, Abilene knew the flurry of activity she was feeling in her own system at the sight of this man—the increased heart rate, the shortness of breath, the *instant* arousal—was happening to him, too.

"You came," he whispered.

She blushed at his word choice, and he noticed, his cheeks dotting with their own flush of color.

"Again with this notion that I had a choice in the matter," Abilene said, not as sternly as she would have hoped.

Eli's brows drew together. He looked confused, as though he didn't know she was not here under her own power.

"I had a military escort," she said.

Eli's expression turned into a dangerous glower in the span of one of her frantic heartbeats. He took another step toward her. "They forced you here? I want the name of every soldier who put his hands on you."

Abilene sucked in a breath. She'd forgotten how intensely this man guarded her. She'd forgotten how amazing it felt to be cared for so ferociously.

She shook her head once. "No one hurt me," she assured him. His glower went down in intensity only slightly, and Abilene was warmed all over again.

She offered him an awkward smile. Coming into this office had been a mistake. She was doomed. She should have turned and walked away the moment her heart told her Eli was here when she'd first come into the building.

She had tenuous control over her traitorous body. Her mind was screaming for her to launch herself into his arms and wrap her body around his.

Her knees grew weak at the idea.

Want. I want so bad, the primitive part of her brain piped up.

The silence between them became too awkward for Eli to handle. "Please come to work for us, Abilene," he said so, so softly. "I know we don't deserve someone of your scientific caliber, but it would put this Operation on solid ground. We need you."

His confidence in her washed over her like a balm, touching her more deeply than any other person's feelings about her ever had. She closed her eyes and basked in the glow of his inadvertent praise.

Eli continued talking. "We kept your name out of everything, Abilene, I swear. No one here knows of what happened with Major Taylor, or that," he swallowed, "you were forced to take the fruit."

His voice dripped with sorrow and regret at this latest. "And no one, *no one*, will ever know of our . . . i-interaction. I promise."

He'd protected her even in her absence. Protected her completely. She realized with a start that she had never once questioned what would happen to her if the authorities found out she had killed Major Taylor. She had known that she would never be connected to that incident. That Eli would always ensure her safety.

"I'll do whatever it takes," Eli whispered, "to work with a genius like you."

She winced. *Genius* was as bad as *perfect.* "I'm only human, Eli. Not a genius. Not perfect. Just Abilene."

Comprehension dawned on his face. "I've always known that, Abilene. You think with a temper like yours I would have ever mistaken you for perfect? And you snore. Pretty loudly."

She gasped in outrage. He chuckled.

He took another step toward her. "And you eat McDonalds every meal you can."

He was in front of her now. She could smell the soap he used. Feel his body heat. She swayed toward him.

"And you have the most beautiful eyes I've ever seen. You care for the people in your life with formidable courage. You hold others accountable for their actions and *force* them to be better people. You drive me out of my head with lust."

His blunt fingers moved to brush her cheek. "And I was the worst kind of idiot to ever think you were something other than who you are: the woman I can't live without."

An embarrassingly loud sob escaped Abilene, and she was pulled into Eli's crushing embrace a second later.

He felt *so* good. He arms were tight and firm around her. Her hands clutched at the muscles of his back as she buried her nose in his wide chest and cried, and cried, and cried.

His murmured sentiments rumbled through his body, and one of his hands moved to the back of her head to finger-comb her curls. He held her for what seemed an endless amount of time as his words, his actions, his character worked to heal years of Abilene's hurt.

"Abilene, I've missed you so much," he whispered into her hair. She drew back to look up at him.

"I'm pregnant," she blurted.

He froze. "W-what?"

She nibbled on her bottom lip. "I'm pregnant, Eli. Twelve weeks," she added, lest the stupid male get the wrong idea. *I'm carrying your baby, idiot,* was the subtext.

"I got you pregnant?" he asked.

He'd still shown no emotion. Abilene nodded. She didn't know what she would do if he handled this badly. Her emotions were on a wild roller coaster as it was.

"Ah, God," he groaned, and then she was caught up in his arms again, held more gently this time, and his breath came in ragged bursts. "You're killing me here, woman. How are you going to convince me you're not perfect if you keep making me the happiest man in the world?"

And then he was kissing her. Tenderly. Thoroughly. His tongue stroking into her mouth. His fingers tunneling into her hair. "I love you. So much," he whispered into her mouth.

Abilene melted into his embrace even more. She'd hoped in a million different ways that someday Eli would say and do something to put her back into his arms. The reality far outweighed any of her fantasies. "I love you, too," she whispered back. "I always have. Even when you were an ass."

He smiled into her eyes, but before he could kiss her again, she stopped him with a hand to his chest.

"So, maybe we should go over the company dating policy," she said with a wink.

He chuckled and pulled her closer. "Whatever it is, I'm sure marriage will solve any questions."

Abilene froze and waited for the panic to hit at the idea of being trapped with someone for the rest of her life.

She waited.

And waited.

Eli continued to hold her and stare into her eyes.

And that was when she noticed.

He was looking at her. Really *looking* at her.

He saw her.

It's right, the Voice whispered to her. *This time, it's right.*

Tears flooded her eyes again. "Sorry," she choked, waving a hand in front of her eyes. "Hormones."

He kissed her cheek and one of his hands trailed down her back to cup her ass. "Well, let's see if we can get some different hormones firing, hmm?"

The desire to cry fled. "Bring it on, baby," she whispered.

And he did.

About the Author

Micah Persell holds a bachelor's degree in English and a double master's degree in literature and English pedagogy. She is an avid reader of all types of literature, but has a soft spot for romance. She currently teaches high school language arts classes in California where she lives with her husband, two dogs, and two cats. She loves to answer e-mails and connect with readers on Facebook, Twitter, and Pinterest. Visit her website at *www.micahpersell.com*.

www.ingramcontent.com/pod-product-compliance
Lightning Source LLC
Chambersburg PA
CBHW010638100726
47900CB00011B/2879